Joseph Fitzgerald Molloy

**Famous Plays**

Their Histories and their Authors

Joseph Fitzgerald Molloy

**Famous Plays**
*Their Histories and their Authors*

ISBN/EAN: 9783337280352

Printed in Europe, USA, Canada, Australia, Japan

Cover: Foto ©Andreas Hilbeck / pixelio.de

More available books at **www.hansebooks.com**

# FAMOUS PLAYS.

# FAMOUS PLAYS

*THEIR HISTORIES AND THEIR AUTHORS.*

BY

## J. FITZGERALD MOLLOY,

AUTHOR OF "COURT LIFE BELOW STAIRS," "ROYALTY RESTORED," ETC.

*NEW EDITION.*

LONDON:

WARD & DOWNEY,

12, YORK STREET, COVENT GARDEN, W.C.

1888

# HENRY IRVING, Esq.

---

DEAR MR. IRVING,

Since Garrick died, no player has studied more persistently or laboured more strenuously to elevate the stage than you. Your intelligence, inventiveness, and genius, as student, manager, and actor, have kept the highest form of histrionic art vigorous and fruitful among us. Through your ingenious powers and liberal enterprise the dramatist of all time has in the present age been familiarised to his countrymen ; the greatest English poet of our day has been accepted as a playwright. Your scholarly conceptions and powerful representations have inspired new schools of acting, and have justly rendered you the recipient of weighed admiration, wrested from an unemotional age, and wrung from an unimaginative nation. Your stage has become the sanctuary of art, your theatre the home of culture.

That this volume is not more worthy your acceptance, is to me a cause of regret ; that it bears your name, a source of satisfaction.

Believe me,

Faithfully yours always,

J. FITZGERALD MOLLOY.

*September*, 1886.

# PREFACE.

FOR knowledge of the playhouses which obtained under the Restoration, all students of dramatic history are dependent on Roscius Anglicanus, a small, imperfect volume written by John Downes, book-keeper and prompter to the Duke's Company from 1662 to 1706. Concerning the patents granted by Charles II. to Killigrew and Davenant, for the establishment of their respective theatres, Downes confines himself to two sentences. A great part of his book of fifty-two pages is occupied by a list of plays and their respective casts, performed by both companies under these managers. Of the Drury Lane or King's company of comedians, his account is most brief, his knowledge of them being received from Charles Booth, "some time book-keeper there." If Downes deviates, "he begs pardon of the reader and subscribes himself his very humble servant," a proceeding which, if courteous, is unsatisfactory.

Genest's information regarding this period of stage history is mainly derived from Downes, and is therefore meagre and incomplete. Malone's History of the English Stage is valuable from copies of deeds it contains concerning the patents, but is diffuse, and makes little mention of minor details. All information possibly obtainable and wholly reliable I have gathered from Downes, Malone, the valuable documents printed by the Shakespeare Society, as likewise from volumes mentioned in the first part of the appended list of books consulted. In all, the paper prefixing this volume will be found to contain the first concise and exact account of the Restoration playhouses yet printed.

A narration of circumstances under which the plays selected were written and produced, is given without attempt at criticising their merits. When contemporary notices of these productions appeared, extracts from them are given; at some length in the case of Lord Lytton's dramas, as doubtless it will be interesting to compare press opinions greeting their first appearances with criticisms afterwards elicited. Some details concerning the authors of these plays are added, from belief that personality ever entertains, and in hope verbal outlines will help readers to complete mental pictures of the personages and their works mentioned in these pages.

J. FITZGERALD MOLLOY.

# A LIST OF THE BOOKS AND PAMPHLETS CONSULTED IN WRITING THIS VOLUME.

---

A COLLECTION of Materials towards an History of the English Stage; Prynne's Histrio-Mastix; Stubbes' Anatomy of Abuses; William Cooke's Elements of Dramatic Criticism; Shakespeare Society Papers; Malone's Historical Account of the Rise and Progress of the 'English Stage; Langburne's Account of English Dramatic Poets; Momus Triumphanus; Dane's Dramatic Miscellanies; Downes' Roscius Anglicanus; Betterton's History of the English Stage; Halliwell's Dictionary of Old Plays; Charles Dibden's Complete History of the English Stage; Life and Works of Congreve; Letters Written by Congreve; Memorials of English Affairs; Apology for the Life of Colley Cibber; Gilden's Life of Betterton; An Account of Betterton; Buckle's Miscellaneous and Posthumous Works; Denis's Letters upon Several Occasions; Collier's Defence; Spence's Anecdotes; Some Account of the Life and Writings of Joseph Addison; Johnson's Life of Addison; Addisoniana; A Letter from Italy to Lord Halifax; Cato, a Tragedy; The Narrative of Dr. Richard Norris Concerning the Frenzy of Mr. John Dennis; Dennis's Remarks of Cato; Mrs. Inchbald's Remarks on Cato; Letters of Mr. Addison and Mr. Pope; Memoir of Joseph Addison, with a Particular Account of His Writings; Anderson's Life of

Gay; The Beggar's Opera; Johnson's Life of Gay; Dean
Swift's Literary Correspondence; Pope's Letters; Horace
Walpole's Letters; Boswell's Life of Johnson; Dr. Percy's
Life of Goldsmith; Peake's Memoirs of the Colman Family;
Northcote's Life of Reynolds, and Conversations; Sir James
Prior's Life of Goldsmith; Cradock's Memoirs of Gold-
smith; Arthur Murphy's Life of Garrick; Davies' Life of
Garrick; Sheridan's Life and Times; Sheridaniana; Wat-
kins' Memoirs of the Private Life of Sheridan; Moore's
Life of Sheridan; Le Fanu's Memoir of Sheridan; Authentic
Memoirs of Sheridan; Reynolds' Life and Times; Wood's
Personal Recollections of the Stage; Wemyss' Theatrical
Biography; Hodder's Memoirs of My Time; Bernard's
Retrospection of the Stage; Life of James Sheridan
Knowles; Planche's Recollections and Reflections;
Hawkins' Life of Kean; Phippen's Memoirs of Kean;
Fanny Kemble's Records; Hazlitt's Personal Recollections;
Short View of the English Stage, and Spirit of the Age;
Macready's Reminiscences; Lord Lytton's Life and Letters;
Scharf's Recollections of Scenic Effects; Lord Lytton's
Dramas; Harriet Martineau's Autobiography; William
Jerdan's Personal Reminiscences and Men I have Known;
Leigh Hunt's Recollections of Writers; Charles Knight's
Passages of a Working Life; Forster's Life of Dickens.

# CONTENTS.

Macready Meets Bulwer—The Actor Makes a Suggestion—*The Duchess de la Vallière*—First Representation—Unfavourable Reception—*The Lady of Lyons*—Curiosity of the Town—The Plot of an Historical Drama—Letters from the Playwright—*Richelieu* in the Greenroom—First Night of *Richelieu*—Criticism of the *Times*—*The Sea Captain*—Macready at the Haymarket—Production of *Money*—First-Night Demonstration—*Not so Bad as We Seem*—*Junius; or, The Household Gods.*

# CONGREVE'S LOVE FOR LOVE.

Revival of Dramatic Representations—Three Companies
Divert the Town—A Royal Patent—The Duke's Com-
pany and their Performances—The King's Company—
Erection of Drury Lane—Destruction by Fire—Rebuilt
by Christopher Wren—A Nursery for Players—Scenery
First Introduced on the English Stage—The First
Opera Performed in England—Contentions of the Rival
Houses—Union of the Companies—Thomas Betterton
—Sore Vexations—A New Theatre and a New Play—
William Congreve—Production of *Love for Love*.

# FAMOUS PLAYS.

## CONGREVE'S LOVE FOR LOVE.

PLAYHOUSES, being regarded as sloughs of ini-
quity by the Puritans, were suppressed during
the Commonwealth. Accordingly, " stages, feats,
and galleries" were demolished, and "all players,
though calling themselves the King's or Queen's
servants," were ordered to be punished as rogues
and vagabonds. At prospect of the Restoration,
the national love of dramatic representations
revived ; and towards the latter part of the
year 1659, such players as had weathered the
hardships and survived the struggles of civil
warfare and despotic rule, coming together
once more, acted at the Red Bull Tavern, in
St. John's Street.

Charles II. landed in May, 1660; and during the ensuing period of general rejoicement three companies of players sought favour of the town, performing respectively at the Cockpit in Drury Lane, at Salisbury Court in Fleet Street, and, as before mentioned, at the Red Bull Tavern, in St. John's Street.

Now, by a royal grant, "the allowance of plays, the ordering of players and playmakers, and the permission for erecting of playhouses, hath time out of minde whereof the memory of man is not to the contrary," belonged to the office of His Majesty's Master of the Revels. And Sir Henry Herbert, resuming that high position on the re-establishment of monarchy, sought to maintain the privileges of his predecessors in office, and secure such fees as had formerly been exacted by them for the exhibition of plays. The managers of these companies, namely Sir William Davenant, William Beeston, and Mr. Rhodes, determining to resist his authority, law-suits ensued; and finally Sir Henry Herbert was obliged to forego his claims. Soon after, his sway over plays and playhouses was completely overthrown by a royal grant concerning them, which passed the Privy Signet on the 21st August, 1660, and the Great Seal in 1663.

This document stated that certain plays and interludes, to which divers citizens resorted for entertainment, containing much matter of profanation and scurrility, and for the most part tending to the debauchery of manners of such as were present, being very scandalous and offensive to all pious and well-disposed persons, the King, believing such entertainments if well managed might serve as moral instructions in human life, now resolved to place them under control of two well-approved good gentlemen. And having experience of the art and skill of his trusty and well-beloved Thomas Killigrew, Esquire, one of the Grooms of his Bedchamber, and of Sir William Davenant, Knight, His Majesty gave and granted unto them full power and authority "to erect two companies of players, consisting respectively of such persons as they shall choose and appoint, and to purchase, builde, and erect, or hire, at their charge, as they shall think fitt, two houses or theatres, with all convenient roomes and other necessaries thereunto appertaining, for the representation of tragydies, comedyes, playes, operas, and all other entertainments of that nature, in convenient places."

They were likewise given power to settle and establish payments for admission that should be reasonable in regard to the great expenses of scenes, music, and such decorations as had not formerly been used; with further permission to make such allowances to actors and other persons employed in the representations as might be considered suitable. And in regard to the extraordinary licentiousness that had lately obtained in theatrical performances, it was His Majesty's pleasure "there should be no more places of representations, nor companies of actors of plays, or operas by recitative, music, or representations by dancing, or any other entertainment on the stage, in the cities of London and Westminster, or in the liberties thereof, save these two erected by his authority."

The patentees were respectively forbidden to act plays, interludes, or operas, containing profanations, scurrility, or obscenity. They were, furthermore, commanded to pursue all plays formerly written, and expunge objectionable passages before they were represented.

The King likewise granted on the 20th of December, 1660, a patent empowering George Jolly, gentleman, "to erect one company, consisting respectively of such as he should choose and appoint, and to purchase, build, or hyre, att his costs and charges, one house or theatre, with all convenient roomes and other necessarys thereunto apperteyneing."

But George Jolly, however, made no use of his warrant, and ultimately disposed of it to Killigrew and Davenant for a certain consideration.

Sir Henry Herbert protested and petitioned against the granting of such patents, as being certain infringements on rights exercised by his office since players were admitted by authority to act. "And it may be of very ill consequence," he adds, in his address to the King, "by a new grant to take away and cut off a branch of your ancient powers, granted to the said office, under the Great Seale." His protest, however, had not the effect desired.

The players governed by Sir William Davenant were known as the Duke's Company. For some time they acted at the Cockpit, in Drury Lane, and at Salisbury Court; from where they moved, in the early part of 1662, to a new theatre in Portugal Row, near Lincoln's Inn Fields.

Here they drew crowded houses daily. John Downes, who from 1662 to 1706 continued their book-keeper and prompter, "writing out all the parts in each play, and attending every morning the actors' rehearsals, and their performances in afternoons," in speaking of their various performances tells us, "no succeeding tragedy for several years got more reputation or money to the company" than *Hamlet*. The *rôle* of the melancholy Dane was represented by Thomas Betterton. Sir William Davenant had seen Taylor, who had been instructed by Shakespeare in the part, and the traditions handed down by the poet were bequeathed to Betterton, whose exact performance, Downes states, "gained him esteem and reputation superlative to all other plays."

Another representation which secured the company "great gain and estimation from the town," was *Love and Honour*, written by Sir William Davenant, who had succeeded rare Ben Jonson as poet laureate to Charles I., and at the Restoration had resumed that office in the court of Charles II. This tragi-comedy was richly dressed—the King giving his coronation suit to Betterton, who played Prince Alvaro; the Duke of York his to Harris, who represented Prince Prospero; and my Lord Oxford his habit to Price, who enacted the Duke of Parma's son.

*Romeo and Juliet* was another performance which drew great houses. Mr. James Howard, an ingenious gentleman, converted the play into a tragi-comedy, in which the lovers were made happy in the last act. This was played alternately with the tragedy as written by Shakespeare, for several consecutive days; each enjoying success. Sir George Etheridge's *Love in a Tub* was likewise much admired. "The clean and well performance of this comedy," writes Downes, "got the company more reputation and profit than any preceding comedy, the company taking in a month's time at it £1,000."

The full tide of success enjoyed by Davenant's players was interrupted by the fatal plague in 1656, and the calamitous fire of the following year.* But the effect of these visitations passing away, public spirit again revived, and crowds resorted once more to the Lincoln's Inn Fields Theatre. This becoming insufficient to accommodate the audiences which flocked there, Sir William Davenant built a playhouse in Dorset Gardens, to where his company removed in 1671. On the 9th November the new house opened with the performance of Dryden's comedy, *Sir Martin Marall*, which continued acting, says John Downes, "three days together, with a full audience each day, notwithstanding it had been acted thirty days before in Lincoln's Inn Fields, and above four times at court."

The players under Killigrew's management were known as the King's Company, or His Majesty's Servants. Ten of them were enrolled upon the royal household establishment, wore

---

* See Royalty Restored, vol. II. chap. i.

a uniform of scarlet cloth and gold lace, and were set down by the Lord Chamberlain as Gentlemen of the Bedchamber. From the year 1660 until 1663, they played in Gibbon's Tennis Court, in Vere Street, near Clare Market, whilst a theatre was being erected for them in Drury Lane, at a cost of fifteen hundred pounds. This building measured one hundred and twelve feet in length from east to west, and fifty-nine feet in breadth from north to south. The new house was opened on Thursday, the 8th of April, 1663, with Beaumont and Fletcher's *Humorous Lieutenant,* which ran for twelve consecutive days. Nine years later, in January, 1672, the theatre was wholly destroyed by fire, as were likewise above fifty houses adjoining it, some being burnt, and others blasted to prevent the flames spreading.

Thereon the King's Servants removed to the playhouse in Lincoln's Inn Fields, which had been vacated by the Duke's Company. Meanwhile a new theatre, built upon plans furnished by Sir Christopher Wren, and costing the sum of four thousand pounds, was being erected

by Killigrew and his company,* on the ruins
of the old and site of the present Drury Lane
Theatre, "between Drury Lane and Bridges
Streete, in the parish of St. Martin-in-the-Fields,
and of St. Paul's, Covent Garden, or one of
them, in the county of Middlesex."

The King's Company played here for the
first time on the 26th March, 1674.

Inasmuch as both houses equally divided
the interests of the town, perfect harmony existed
between them for a while. A rule was made
and observed, that a piece performed at one
theatre should not be attempted at the other.
The plays of Shakespeare, Beaumont and Fletcher,
Jonson, and Shorley were by alternate choice,
and with approbation of the court, divided

---

* The copy of a curious and interesting deed, dated
1673, is printed in the Shakespeare Society's Papers, vol. iv.
p. 147, relative to "one hundred and three score pounds"
advanced by Nicholas Burt, or Burght, member of the
King's Company, for "the makeing and providing of scenes,
machines, cloathes, apparell, and other things to be used
in, or relating to the acting of comedies, tragedies, and
other interludes at the said theatre, or at any place where
the company associated, or to be associated, for such acting,
shall act."

between the companies. Nor were the rival players yet troubled by the spirit of envy.

Betterton, of the Duke's Company, was famous for his personation of Hamlet; whilst Charles Hart, * grand-nephew of Shakespeare, drew crowded houses to Drury Lane by his representation of Othello. The town, holding each theatre in equal esteem, was liberal in supporting both. The general enthusiasm which obtained regarding them was not alone a vigorous reaction from the solemnity of Puritanism; for general curiosity was excited to witness the performances of women, now introduced upon the English stage for the first time, female parts having previously been played by young men and boys of feminine appearances, dressed in the costumes of women.

That these prosperous companies might not in course of time lack excellent players, His Majesty,

---

* Rymer, in his Tragedies of the Last Age Considered, says of Hart : "The eyes of the audience are prepossessed and charmed by his action, before aught of the poet can approach their ears, and to the most wretched of characters he gives a lustre which dazzles the sight, that the deformities of the poet cannot be perceived."

on the 30th March, 1665, at the petition of Thomas
Killigrew and Sir William Davenant, granted
a patent to William Legg, one of the Grooms
of the Bedchamber (ancestor to the present
Earl of Dartmouth), whereby he was vested
with "power, liberty, licence, and authoritie to
erect and make a theatre, and to gather together
boyes and girles and others to be instructed, in
the nature of a nursery, for the trayneing upp
of persons to act playes, to bee from time to
time approved by the said Thomas Killigrew
and Sir William Davenant, that they may out
of the said company take out actors, and remove the said boyes and girles and other actors
soe to bee there instructed, for the supply of
each of their said companyes as shall bee meete."

Therefore William Legg was granted permission to "lawfully, peacably, and quietly frame,
erect, and new build, and set upp, or otherwise purchase or procure, in any place within
our citties of London and Westminster, or the
suburbes thereof, wherein hee or they shall find
best accomodation for that purpose, to bee
assigned and allotted out or approved by the

surveyor of our workes for the time being, one theatre or playhouse, with such necessary tyreing and retyreing rooms and other places convenient, of such extent and dimensions as hee or they shall thinke fitting, wherein tragedies, comedies, playes, operas, musique, sceanes, and all other entertainments of the stage whatsoever, may be showed and presented."

William Legg's company was also permitted "to act playes and entertainments of the stage of all sorts, peacably and quietly, without the impeachment or impediment of any person or persons whatsoever, for the recreation of such as shall desire to see the same; and that itt shall be lawful for the said William Legg, his heirs and assignes, to take and receive of such as shall resort to see or hear any such playes, sceanes, and entertainment whatsoever, such summe or summes of money as have bin heretofore given or taken in the like kind."

The interesting document from which information concerning the nursery is gathered was presented in 1847 by Mr. Thomas Edlyne Tomlins to the Shakespeare Society, who published it amongst their papers in the same year. It is not a little remarkable that no mention of this school is made by John Downes in his *Roscius Anglicanus*; or, Historical Review of the Stage from 1660 to 1706. That it existed is, however, proved by references made to it by Langbaine, who, in his Account of Dramatic Poets, records having first seen Chapman's *Revenge for Honour* acted "at the Nursery." Moreover, John Dryden, in his poem, " McFlecknoe," speaking of Barbican and certain houses standing in the vicinity, says :

Near those a nursery erects its head,
Where queens are form'd, and future heroes bred ;
Where unfledg'd actors learn to laugh and cry,
And little Maximins the gods defy.

Gaining recruits from this school, the new theatres prospered exceedingly, popularity being secured by the excellent acting witnessed at either house, as well as by new plays and witty, which succeeded each other rapidly in this age of intellectual brilliancy. But the players chiefly owed prosperity to the court, of which they became a means of delight and

source of interest; for not only did royalty lend its
presence to their various performances, but likewise betrayed its interest in their private concerns,
so that all differences and complaints were submitted to, and decided by, the King or his
brother. This happy condition continued for
upwards of ten years, when a change was
gradually effected. The King's Servants gaining
new recruits, drew greater audiences to witness
their achievements; jealous of which, the Duke's
Company, in addition to the regular plays, introduced dramatic operas, embellished not only
with dancing and singing, but gorgeous decorations, costly apparel, and ingenious machinery.
Sir William Davenant had, indeed, been the first
to introduce scenery upon the English stage.
Having been for some time imprisoned during
the Commonwealth, he was discharged towards
the end of Cromwell's reign. On regaining his
liberty he, notwithstanding the troubled times,
became anxious to have one of his productions,
*The Siege of Rhodes*, performed as an opera, and
being a bold man, shaped his desires to words,
and in the following manner addressed Sir

c

Bulstrode Whitelock, a lover of art, himself a composer, who had gained favour with Cromwell, and held the office of Commissioner of the Treasury under the Protectorate :

"My Lord,

    " When I consider the nicety of the times, I fear it may draw a curtain between your lordship and our opera ; therefore I have presumed to send your lordship, hot from the press, what we mean to represent, making your lordship my supreme judge, though I despair to have the honour of inviting you to be a spectator.   I do not conceive the perusal of it worthy any part of your lordship's leisure, unless your ancient relation to the Muses make you not unwilling to give a little entertainment to poetry ; though in so mean a dress as this, and coming from, my lord,

        " Your lordship's most obedient servant,

            " WILLIAM  DAVENANT."

This letter, received by Sir Bulstrode Whitelock in September, 1656, two years before the death of Cromwell, and four years previous to the Restoration, is published in Memorials of the

English Affairs from the Beginning of the Reign of Charles the First to the Happy Restoration of King Charles the Second, vol. iv. p. 273. It was certainly a sign of the coming time that he was permitted to perform his opera. In a biographical sketch of Davenant, published in Mason's Historical Account of the English Stage, it is written: "Because plays (*scil.* trage. and comedies) were in those Presbyterian times scandalous, he contrives to set up an opera, *stylo recitativo:* wherein Serjeant Maynard and several citizens were engagers; it began at Rutland House in Charterhouse Yard; next, at the Cockpit in Drury Lane, where were acted very well, *stylo recitativo, Sir Francis Drake* and *The Seige of Rhodes,* 1st and 2nd part. It did affect the eie and eare extremely. This first brought scenes in fashion in England: before at plays was only an hanging."* *The Siege of Rhodes* was certainly

---

* An attempt at scenery had previously been made in the reign of James I., who, whilst being entertained at Oxford in 1605, witnessed the performance of three plays in the hall of Christ Church. According to the "Leland Collect," the scenery was designed by no less a personage than Inigo Jones. The following description of it is

the first opera performed in England.  In a note contained in the Memorials, it is mentioned : " Sir William Davenant printed his opera, notwithstanding the nicety of the times."  The full title of this production was " *The Seige of Rhodes*, made a Representation by the Art of Prospective in Scenes ; and the Story sung in Recitative Musick, at the back part of Rutland House, in the upper end of Aldersgate Street, London." Copies were " printed in 1656, for Henry Herringham, and are to be sold at his shop, at the sign of the Anchor, on the Lower Walk, in the New Exchange."

The fashion established in introducing scenery, was, after Sir William Davenant's demise in 1688, followed by his son, Dr. Charles Davenant, who succeeded him as patentee and manager.  In 1673 he produced, as Downes narrates, " *The Tempest ; or, the Enchanted Island*, made into an opera by Mr.

---

given : " The stage was built close to the upper end of the hall, as it seemed at the first sight ; but indeed it was but a false wall faire painted, and adorned with stately pillars, which pillars would turn about ; by reason whereof, with the help of other painted clothes, their stage did vary three times in the acting of one tragedy."

Shadwell, having all new in it: as scenes, machines; particularly one scene, painted with myriads of ariel spirits; and another flying away with a table furnished out with fruits, sweetmeats, and all sorts of viands, just when the Duke Trinculo and his companions were going to dinner." Under Dr. Davenant's management, *Macbeth* was set on the stage with great finery and "machines as flyings for the witches;" whilst the opera of *Psyche* "came forth in all her ornaments, new scenes, new machines, new cloathes," which cost over eight hundred pounds. Another opera, *The Tempest*, altered by Dryden and Davenant, was set forth with great musical attractions, as may be judged from directions contained in the printed copy, to "the band of twenty-four violins, with the harpsicals and theorbos which accompany the voices."

Mere operas, mounted with costly scenery, drew the town from the King's Company. Rivalry and bitterness therefore sprang up between them. Pieces called *The Mock Tempest* and *Psyche Debauched* were produced at the opposition house, when not only the operas were parodied, but the actors imitated. In a witty prologue spoken at the opening of Drury Lane, in 1764, Dryden, referring to the innovation made by the Duke's Company, says:

> I would not prophecy our house's fate : '
> But while vain shows and scenes you over-rate
> 'Tis to be feared—
> That, as a fire the former house overthrew,
> Machines, and tempests will destroy the new.

The evil accruing from this rivalry to each soon became plain to both, and although Betterton, being the principal member of the Duke's Company, suggested they should mutually cease hostilities, unite their efforts, and act in one house, the Drury Lane company, considering themselves superior to their rivals, were not prepared to heed this project. Therefore in order to gain their desires, Dr. Charles Davenant, together with Thomas Betterton and William Smith, the principal members of his company, resolved to weaken the forces and humble the pride of their opponents. Accordingly, doubtless believing all was fair in love and war, they entered into an agreement with Charles Hart and Edward Kynaston, the chief players of His Majesty's troop, to leave their fellows. In a memorandum, dated October 14th, 1681, contained in Gildon's Life of Betterton, Dr. Davenant, Thomas Betterton, and William Smith agreed to pay, " or cause to be paid out of the profits of acting, unto Charles Hart and Edward Kynaston, five shillings apiece for every day there shall be any tragedies or comedies, or other representations acted at the Duke's Theatre in Salisbury Court, or wherever the company shall act during the respective lives of the said Charles Hart and Edward Kynaston, excepting the days the young men and women play for their own profit only. But this agreement to cease if the said Charles Hart or Edward Kynaston shall at any time play among or effectually assist the King's Company of actors, and for so long as this is paid, they both covenant and promise not to play at the King's Theatre."

In consideration of their pensions, Hart and Kynaston promised to make over unto Dr. Davenant, Betterton, and Smith, "all right, title, and claim which they or either of them may have to any plays, books, cloathes, or scenes in the

King's Playhouse," together with the claim " they or each of them have to six and threepence apiece for every day there shall be any playing at the King's Theatre."

Deprived of two popular actors, the dramatic talent of His Majesty's Servants was considerably weakened ; and after a struggle maintained for about three years, both companies united in 1682, and played in Drury Lane Theatre. By reason of their strength and excellence, they drew great audiences, to which were afforded unbounded satisfaction and delight. And now rapidly developed the genius of the first great English actor, of whom it was said he was born to illustrate Shakespeare, Thomas Betterton. The son of an under-cook in the kitchen of Charles I., he had early in life manifested a taste for polite learning, and in accordance with his desires, was apprenticed to a bookseller named Rhodes, residing at the sign of the Bible in Charing Cross. Now this worthy man had formerly been wardrobe-keeper to the late King's Company of Comedians at Blackfriars ; and though forced by circumstances to abandon his calling, the fascination it had formerly exercised still held possession of him. Therefore, when a change of national events permitted, he established a company of players at the Cockpit, in Drury Lane; two prominent members of which were his apprentices Kynaston, who acted female parts, and Betterton, who personated the heroes of tragedy and comedy. And in due time, when patents were granted to Killigrew and Sir William Davenant, the latter selected all those acting under Rhodes as members of his company, amongst whom was Betterton, who rose rapidly in public esteem. It was not, however, until his removal to Drury Lane, that his great powers were more fully appreciated and generally acknowledged.

His dramatic genius, aided by his commanding presence and melodious voice, surprised and delighted the town. So fully did he engage the admiration of audiences, that, as Colley Cibber states, "upon his entrance into every scene he seemed to seize upon the eyes and ears of the giddy and inadvertent. To have talked or looked another way, would then have been thought insensibility or ignorance!" Anthony Aston adds his testimony that the great actor's voice "forced an universal attention even from fops and orange girls," the common pests of the playhouse. When he personated Hamlet, all laying claim to polite judgment and nice taste flocked to see him ; but his Othello was considered a still more powerful performance. Addison states, " the wonderful agony which he appeared in when he examined the circumstances of the handkerchief, the mixture of love which intruded in his mind upon the innocent answers Desdemona makes, betrayed in his gesture such a variety and vicissitude of passions, as would admonish a man to be afraid of his own heart, and perfectly convince him that it is to stab it, to admit that worst of daggers, jealousy." Nor was he less excellent in comedy ; his airy grace, brilliant vivacity, and natural acting excelled and fascinated.

His merit was indeed far greater than his reward ; inasmuch as his salary at this time never exceeded four pounds a week. The town now possessing but one theatre, its actors were at the mercy of the united patentees, who accordingly imposed what terms they pleased upon them.

By a new arrangement, the receipts were divided into twenty shares, ten of which were appropriated by the management, the remainder being divided amongst the players according to their deserts. And presently the patentees' allotments being sold to speculators, their owners, no matter how great their ignorance and incapacity might be, were permitted to participate in the direction of the theatre. Harassed by many masters, treated with injustice, and regarded with contempt, the poor players were sorely grieved ; and when those prominent amongst them complained of hardships to which they were subjected, their parts were taken from them and given to young and incapable performers. Moreover, the new management reintroduced dramatic operas, on which were lavished vast sums ; and these proving successful, the actors of legitimate pieces were held in greater disregard than before. Nor was this all, for sums expended on the operas falling due, it was resolved, by way of meeting them, to further reduce the players' slender incomes. Writhing under many wrongs, Betterton re-

monstrated with the managers ; but his objection
to their conduct seemed as treason to their
government.    Therefore, his words having no
avail, he resolved to free himself, and those who
would join him, from the hated yoke which
oppressed them ; and, gaining over the principal
performers, they left the theatre, resolving to
rise or fall together.    And their grievances
becoming a general topic of the town, they
gained the sympathy and approval of all classes.

Charles II., of gracious memory, who had
ever regarded his servants with kindly interest,
was no more.    His brother James, who had
likewise aided and favoured them, was banished,
and William and Mary occupied the throne.
The players now designed to gain their sovereign's
interest, and this they eventually succeeded in
obtaining through the clemency of the Lord
Chamberlain, the Earl of Dorset, who has been
described as "a favourite, friend, and protector
of the Muses." Nay, William of Orange granted
them an audience, when, laying bare their
wrongs to his sight, they besought protection
of his justice.    In answer he dismissed them

with assurances of firm support and speedy relief. Therefore a royal license was granted, empowering them to act in a separate theatre. Accordingly they set about building themselves a house, and selected the tennis court in Lincoln's Inn Fields as a most suitable site. And those who had before sympathised with their cause now subscribed liberally towards erecting the new building, which was completed in 1695. It then became desirable an original play, which would serve to exhibit Betterton and his followers to the best advantage, should be secured for the opening night. Fortunately this lay ready to their hands in the comedy of *Love for Love*, by William Congreve, a young and ingenious playwright, well known to the town.

This young gentleman, who was born in February, 1670, " derived himself from an ancient family," the Congreves of Congreve and Stretton, in Staffordshire. Some time after his birth he was carried to Ireland, where his father, an officer in the army, was then stationed. The future dramatist was educated at Kilkenny, and subsequently at Trinity College, Dublin. On leaving

the university he travelled to London, and entered
himself as a student of law at the Middle Temple.
The career of a lawyer affording him little
interest, he turned his attention to the study of
letters.  A lad of unusual abilities, he had given
promise of developing into a man of ingenious
talents.  At the age of seventeen he had written
a novel, Incognita ; or, Love and Duty Recon-
ciled, which was published when he came of
age.  Though showing considerable merit, it by
no means achieved a success like that awarded
his first play, *The Old Bachelor*, produced in 1693.
This comedy, he avows, was written several years
before its production, by way of amusement during
his recovery from illness.  When finished, he submitted it to the approval of three friends, John
Dryden, Arthur Maynwaring, and Captain Sothern,
who read it with wonder and praised it with
delight.  Seldom had a comedy sparkled with
such brilliant wit, glowed with more exuberant
fancy, or moved with brisker motion.  Dryden
declared he had never seen such a first play in
his life ; but, believing it not quite suitable
for the stage, and fearing it might fail for need

of alteration, he offered to revise it. When his suggestions had been adopted, it was carried to Drury Lane Theatre, where Congreve read it to the manager and his players, but in so indifferent a manner that few hopes of its success were enter-tained. However, on examining the manuscript, Davenant came to a conclusion contrary to that first estimated; and so certain was he of its prosperity, and delighted with its writer's talent, that he allowed him "the freedom of the house" some months before the play was produced. Eventually it was received with the greatest applause imaginable, and was the means of making Congreve's fortune. For George Saville, first Marquis of Halifax, a Lord of the Treasury, being struck with its author's ability, resolved he should be rendered independent to the necessity of hasty productions. He therefore made him a Commissioner for the Licensing of Hackney Coaches.* Subse-

---

* "The salaries of Commissioners for Licensing of Hackney and Stage Coaches being reduced to one hundred pounds per annum, Mr. Ashurst, Mr. Overbury, and Mr. Isham resigned their places, and are to be succeeded by Mr. Herne, Mr. Clark, and Mr. Congreve."—*Post Boy,* June 4, 1693.

quently the same generous patron gave him a post in the Custom House, which secured him six hundred a year.

He was now an author of distinction, " and was able to name among his friends," as Johnson writes, "every man of his time whom wit or elegance had raised to reputation." His sprightly conversation, humorous anecdotes, and love of pleasure made his companionship no less desirable to men, than his handsome presence, vast politeness, and ardent gallantry rendered his society delightful to women. Attired in a square-cut, claret-coloured coat, boasting cuffs of fine linen, garnished with ruffles, a waistcoat reaching the knee, bright-hued stockings, and high-heeled shoes, wearing a flowing peruke and a gold-laced hat, and carrying an orange-scented handkerchief and a tasselled cane, he fluttered airily from the haunts of genius to the abodes of fashion; gossiping in coffee-houses, or dining in taverns with men of parts, flirting at the playhouse, or supping in the homes of ladies of quality.

But, though following pleasure, he loved labour,

and in 1694 produced his second comedy, *The
Double Dealer*; but, though a more entertaining
play, it was not so successful as his first.
However, it by no means lessened his reputation.
Now when it became known *Love for Love* was
to open the Lincoln's Inn Fields Theatre, the
town was filled with curiosity and eagerness to
witness its performance. The comedy had been
read and accepted by the managers of Drury
Lane; but the rupture in the company taking
place, Congreve sympathised with Betterton
and his friends, and gave them his play. On
the afternoon of its first representation the whole
town was astir; coffee-houses and taverns round
Covent Garden were deserted; the King's coach
rolled noisily on its way towards Lincoln's Inn
Fields playhouse, all approaches to which were
already blocked by carriages and sedan chairs,
courtiers and citizens, a noisy, bustling crowd in
all. And presently, the house being filled to
excess, the curtain drew up, and Betterton stepped
forward to read the prologue, and receive a
tumultuous greeting. This excellent actor, together with Mrs. Bracegirdle, who spoke the

D

epilogue, played the parts of Valentine and Angelica, the hero and heroine of the comedy.* The plot was intricate, the situations humorous, the dialogue brilliant, so that its success was assured from its birth. No contemporary criticism of the play is extant; but Dr. Johnson mentions it was "received with more benevolence" than any other of Congreve's works; and the author speaks of "the kind reception it had from the town."† Moreover Downes states the comedy ran for thirteen consecutive days, a certain proof of popularity; for in those times the generality of plays were either, as Tom Brown of Shiffnal writes, "troubled with convulsive fits and died the first night of representation, or by mere dint of acting, held out to the third, which is like a consumptive man's living by cordials, or else

---

* The remaining characters in the cast were filled as follows: Scandall, Mr. Smith; Foresight, Mr. Sandford; Sampson, Mr. Underhill; Ben, Mr. Dogget; Jeremy, Mr. Bourn; Mrs. Frail, Mrs. Barry; Tattle, Mrs. Boman.

† Langbaine states: "The play, though a very good comedy in itself, had this advantage, that it was acted at the opening of the new house, when the town was so prepossessed of the very actors, that before a word was spoken each actor was clapt for a considerable time."

die a violent death, and are interred with the solemnity of cat-calls."

A more substantial proof of the success of *Love for Love* was, the players offered its author a share in the theatre, in consideration of which he was bound, if health permitted, to give them a new play every year.

# ADDISON'S CATO.

FIRST PRODUCED, 14TH APRIL, 1713.

Mr. Joseph Addison Abroad—His Talents as a Poet Render Him Suitable for a Government Post—An Unfinished Tragedy—Honest Dick Steele—Colley Cibber's Opinion of the Piece—Dean Swift at Buttons'—Addison's Introduction to Pope—Political Factions—The Stage and the State—A First Night—An Author's Terror—Success of the Tragedy—Criticisms of Dennis.

# ADDISON'S CATO.

DEATH had not relieved Queen Anne from her troubles, when Addison's famous tragedy, *Cato,* was produced. The grim spectre was, however, within a few months' journey of the royal throne when the play was first witnessed — a fact pregnant with importance in connection with its fate. Years previously it had been conceived and partially written, when Mr. Joseph Addison, the son of a Wiltshire clergyman, was travelling abroad for the purpose of cultivating his mind, improving his manners, and qualifying himself to serve King William III.; for which laudable purposes royalty allowed him the sum of. three hundred pounds per annum.

With the King's death in 1702, Addison's pension ceased. He therefore became tutor to a travelling English squire, a position which brought him but little good fortune; for twelve months after His Majesty's decease, the accomplished scholar returned to England "with a meanness of appearance," as Dr. Johnson writes, "which gave testimony of the difficulties to which he had been reduced." This state of indigence was not destined to be of long continuance. Mr. Addison had by this time acquired arts beseeming a courtier, and waited but an opportunity to render them serviceable. Nor had he long to bide. In 1704, by reason of his talents, he was considered by Lord Halifax the one individual in the kingdom most fit and proper to celebrate the great victory of Blenheim in heroic verse. The task was therefore entrusted him, and the verses he furnished were pronounced equal to his subject. The poet was accordingly awarded an appointment as Commissioner of Appeals; the first of a series of Government posts he was subsequently destined to fill. Here Addison and poverty parted for ever.

On his return from the continent he had

brought with him the first four acts of a tragedy, which at this time he had no thought of placing on the stage. For all that, the accomplished author was not satisfied to hide the light of his genius under a bushel of obscurity, and therefore showed his play, according to Johnson, "to such as were likely to spread their admiration." Foremost amongst these was honest Dick Steele—afterwards Sir Richard—a writer of vigorous prose, a fellow of sprightliest wit, a lover of excellent wine, and a boon companion of many endearments. A schoolfellow of Addison's, their friendship had begun at the Charter House, strengthened at Oxford, and matured in subsequent associations. " I look upon my intimacy with you as one of the most valuable enjoyments of my life," Steele writes to Addison in a letter prefixed to his play of *The Tender Husband;* and in various epistles written to friends the honest fellow bears constant testimony to the same happy affection. Now no man was more willing, and few men were better calculated to spread the fame of Mr. Addison's tragedy than this

loyal friend, this habitué of coffee-houses and
taverns, this intimate of wits and men of parts;
nor was Mr. Addison at all averse to have
his talents so well and loyally advertised.

Twelve months after the author's home-com-
ing, and nine years before *Cato* was produced,
this "best-natured creature in the world," as Dr.
Young terms Steele, carried the first four acts
of *Cato* to no less a personage than Colley
Cibber, actor, author, and joint manager of Drury
Lane Theatre. Colley's pleasure on reading the
manuscripts was exceeding great; indeed he
found himself unable to lay them out of his hands
until he had reached the last line, a fact which
gave Steele such delight as it "was impossible
to dwell upon." The manager's uncommon
satisfaction was, however, somewhat abated on
learning from Steele it was not given him to
produce on the boards of Drury Lane; and
"whatever spirit Mr. Addison had shown in
his writing it, he doubted he would never
have courage enough to let his *Cato* stand the
censure of an English audience; that it had
only been the amusement of his leisure hours

in Italy, and was never intended for the stage."
"This poetical diffidence," says Cibber, "Steele
himself spoke of with some concern, and in the
transport of his imagination could not help
saying, 'Good God, what a part Betterton would
make of Cato!'" It may be noted here the
feeling Colley Cibber spoke of as "poetical
diffidence," Dr. Johnson vigorously described as
"the despicable cant of literary modesty."

That Addison had written the greater part
of a tragedy was now an open secret to his
friends, who were both numerous and distinguished. He had soon after his return been
elected member of the famous Kit Kat Club,
situated in Shire Lane, at the sign of the Cat
and Fiddle. Here at the weekly dinner of
members, over savoury mutton pies and bottles
of excellent port, my Lords Somerset, Grafton,
Richmond, and Kingston schemed an overthrow
of the Tories, Dick Steele sang his merriest song,
Congreve told his raciest story, Vanbrugh discussed
the plots of his comedies, and Dr. Garth sparkled
over with delicious wit. Addison was in those
good days, before unhappy fate united him to

misery and the Countess of Warwick, a social spirit, and as Lady Mary Wortley Montagu says, "the best company in the world." The knowledge he had acquired by continual study, the grace he had gained by foreign travel, rendered him an associate eagerly courted by men of parts; and when "he began to be in company," as Dr. Young quaintly narrates, "he was full of vivacity and went on in a noble stream of thought and language, so as to chain the attention of every one to him." Pope, speaking of the manner in which Addison passed his days at this time, says he spent the mornings in study, then breakfasted with one of his friends, Steele or Philips, Budgell or Colonel Brett, at his lodgings in St. James's Place, "dined at taverns with them, then to Buttons', and then to some tavern again for supper in the evening."

Buttons', situated over against Toms' in Covent Garden, was a favourite resort, not only of Addison's, but of men of letters and fashion, just as Wills' had been a little while before in the days of Dryden. Here politicians held each other in discourse by the button, the

last new satire was repeated, the most recent
pamphlet discussed, the latest play criticised.
Within these precincts, "dukes and other peers
mixed freely with gentlemen, and to be admitted
there needs nothing more than to dress like a
gentleman," as an intelligent foreigner, one Baron
Pollnitz, informs his countrymen. To this coffee-
house, about the year 1704, there constantly
resorted a customer with whose face none of the
habitués were familiar, but from whose pen many
of them had subsequent cause to shrink. By
his gown he was known as a parson, by his
physiognomy he was supposed to be an Irishman.
His features were coarse, his complexion swarthy,
his brows heavy; but his eyes were, as Pope said,
"as azure as the heavens, and had an uncommon
archness in them." His name was Jonathan
Swift.

It was the custom of this parson, on entering
Buttons' house of entertainment, to lay his hat
on a table, and walk backwards and forwards
for half-an-hour or so at a good pace without
speaking to any mortal, or seeming in the least
to notice anything passing around him. He

would then snatch up his hat from the table, dash down his money at the bar, and hasten away. "After having observed this singular behaviour for some time," says Sheridan, who tells the story, "the frequenters of Buttons' concluded him to be out of his senses, and the name that he went by amongst them was that of 'the mad parson.' This made them more than usually attentive to his motions; and one evening, as Mr. Addison and the rest were observing him, they saw him cast his eyes several times on a gentleman in boots, who seemed to be just come out of the country, and at last advance towards him as intending to address him. They were all eager to hear what this dumb mad parson had to say, and immediately quitted their seats to get near him. Swift went up to the country gentleman in a very abrupt manner, and without any previous salute asked him, 'Pray, sir, do you remember any good weather in the world?' The country gentleman, after staring a little at the singularity of his manner and the oddity of the question, answered, 'Yes, sir, thank God, I remember a great deal of good weather in my time.' 'That is more,' said Swift, 'than I can say. I never remember any weather that was not too hot or too cold, too wet or too dry; but however God Almighty contrives it, at the end of the year 'tis all very well.' Upon saying this he took up his hat, and without uttering a syllable more, or taking the least notice of any one, walked out of the coffee-house, leaving all those who had been spectators of this odd scene staring after him, and still more confirmed in the opinion of his being mad."

The Irish parson and the polite scholar soon became intimate, and Addison subsequently declared Swift "the most agreeable companion, the truest friend, and the greatest genius of his age." There can be little doubt the manuscript of *Cato* was submitted to the black-browed parson ; there can be none that it was handed to Mr. Alexander Pope for his special perusal.

Addison had not met this latter poet until about eight years after his first acquaintance with Swift. Pope was then in his twenty-fourth year, whilst Addison was nearing the meridian of his fame as a brilliant essayist and excellent humorist. According to Roscoe, it was Steele who introduced them, and Pope told Spence he liked Addison "as well as he liked any man." He adds that Addison brought *Cato* to him in order to have his sincere opinion of it. This at the end of three or four days Pope gave him : " I told him I thought he had better not act it,' says he, "and that he would get reputation enough by only printing it. This I said as thinking the lines well written, but the piece not theatrical enough."

The four acts of *Cato* were therefore allowed to rest in peace until the first months of the year 1713. It was then considered the time had come, as Johnson writes, "when those who affected to think liberty in danger affected likewise to think that a stage-play might preserve it."

The kingdom had been long divided against itself by two factions, that alternately experienced triumph and defeat, hope and despair. The Tories, headed by Bolingbroke and Oxford, looked anxiously forward to the accession of Her Majesty's brother, James Stuart, sometimes called the Pretender. The Whigs, led by Halifax and Somers, were determined on inviting George Lewis, Elector of Hanover, to reign over the United Kingdoms of Great Britain and Ireland as sovereign lord and king. Childless, though the mother of many children, helpless, though surrounded by numerous advisers, invalided whilst in the meridian of life, Queen Anne was powerless to quell the ferment which raged throughout the nation and found its climax in the capital. Characteristically weak, her conduct had been vacillating. She had commenced by abhorring the Whigs and favouring the Tories, only to dismiss the one in favour of the other. She had honoured and rewarded the great Duke of Marlborough, but to insult and dismiss him. She had loaded Duchess Sarah with favours, to part with her in displeasure. She had sympathised with the unhappy lot of her exiled brother, and had finally issued a proclamation offering a reward for his head, if he were found in Great Britain or Ireland.

With such a feeble-minded monarch on the throne, it was no wonder her subjects were disturbed and disunited. In Ireland, Whigs and Tories frequently ended political disputes in violence and bloodshed; in Scotland, James Stuart's birthday was openly celebrated; whilst in England the populace was in a continued state of agitation. Nowhere was the feeling of disunion more keenly experienced than in London. Politics were the subject of conversation in every club and drawing-room, the object of every toast in public taverns or private dining-rooms, the theme of daily journals and innumerable pamphlets which flooded the town.

Addison having met his first patron in Lord Halifax, a Whig nobleman, had systematically adhered to Whiggism throughout the triumph or defeat of his party; and closely associated with Whig leaders in his official labours and social amusements, they most probably had read scenes or heard passages quoted of his tragedy. And now, with brains heated by party feeling, they had come to imagine some similitude in the history of nations was at hand, between the days when Cato had died in Rome and Anne reigned in

England. The forcible utterances regarding liberty the play contained, was thought by the Whigs, must if the public had an opportunity of hearing them from the stage, bestir the people to a sense of the danger they suffered from the evil machinations of Tories. Accordingly, Addison was besought to finish his tragedy that it might be given to the theatre. The author, however, betrayed a certain reluctance to comply with this request, probably affected, and solicited a friend named Hughes, a dramatist, to add a concluding act to Cato. Delighted with the honour paid him, the grateful playwright hastened on his way and made speedy preparations for reaching the desired end. In a few days he returned with the scenes he had written ; but Addison had meanwhile employed his elegant leisure in composing the required act, and now informed his friend it was half completed.

The tragedy being quite finished was hurried away to Drury Lane playhouse, and speedily prepared for representation. For years past no social event had excited more interest in

town. Political circles looked forward to its effects
with intense anxiety; coffee-house critics hailed
its appearance with uncommon delight, and the
Drury Lane managers regarded it as a probable
source of considerable profit. Addison had
freely and generously declared whatever sum
his play might realise should be theirs, and in
return for such liberality they resolved to mount
its scenes in the handsomest manner possible,
and represent its cast by the best company.
Accordingly the principal characters, Cato, Syphax
and Juba, were played respectively by Booth,
Cibber, and Wilks, whilst the parts of Marcia
and Lucia were entrusted to Mrs. Oldfield and
Mrs. Porter. Barton Booth was a gentleman
by descent, a scholar by education, and an actor
by choice. At the age of seventeen he had
run away from Westminster School, and hired
himself as a player; and six years later had
wooed and wed the daughter of a Norfolk
baronet, Sir William Barkham. With these
leading items in the history of his career, he
was considered an object of interest to the
town at large; with such talents as he exhibited

in pursuit of his calling, he had recommended himself to the managers of Drury Lane as the most suitable representative of Cato. Colley Cibber was of course well known to the play-going world; as was likewise Wilks, who had abandoned "a genteel place under Government" to gratify his passion for acting. Mrs. Oldfield, who has been described as tall, elegant, and well-shaped, was certainly a favourite with the public, and "in sprightliness of air and elegance of manner excelled all others;" whilst Mrs. Porter was declared by one of her contemporary critics "a valuable and respected actress," whose manner exhibited "an elevated consequence which had seldom been equalled."

To render the tragedy furthermore attractive, a stately prologue was written for its production by Alexander Pope, and a humorous epilogue by Dr. Garth. The former, according to the *Guardian*, "prepared the audience for a new scene of passion and transport on a more noble foundation than they have before been entertained with;" the latter, on the same authority, "very agreeably rallied the mercenary traffic between men and women

of this age." All things being ready for the
production of *Cato*, the *Daily Courant* published
the following advertisement, towards the middle
of April, 1713 :

NEVER ACTED BEFORE.

By Her Majesty's Company of Comedians at
the Theatre Royal, in Drury Lane, this present
Tuesday, being the 14 of April, will be presented
the new Tragedy call'd Cato.

When the eventful evening of the first performance arrived, the theatre presented an appearance
of extraordinary brilliancy. Critics, poets, and
players ; students from the Temple ; undergradu-
ates from the universities ; lawyers, doctors, and
men about town were in the pit, most of whom
were friends of Steele's, who was supposed to have
packed the house. There, too, were a band of
citizens under the direction of Sir Gilbert
Heathcote, governor of the Bank of England, a
Whig of the most forward type, who had marched
his men to Drury Lane in case the sturdy Tories
should by reason of their exceeding wickedness

hiss brave Cato's speeches. The boxes were filled with noble peers and their ladies, the rich colouring of whose costumes lent warmth and brightness to the house.

Long before six o'clock, the hour advertised for the play to begin, the theatre was in a state of excitement. Confused murmurs of anxious voices filled the ear; stars on the breasts of peers, and diamonds on the necks of ladies of quality, dazzled the eye. Suddenly the curtain rose, the prologue was spoken amidst breathless silence, and the play began.

A general feeling of enthusiasm rendered the audience far more enthusiastic than critical; and the first of Cato's speeches regarding liberty, was greeted with violent applause from the Whig party on one side of the house, and echoed by uproarious plaudits from Tories on the other. For the latter, to the vast surprise of their opponents, had wisely resolved to turn the tables on their opponents by openly claiming all speeches in favour of liberty as advocating Tory principles, and marking those against tyranny as appropriate to the tenets

of Whigs. This claim on the part of the
Tories to be considered champions of liberty
was furthermore strengthened by a skilful move-
ment of my Lord Bolingbroke's, which, as became its object, was performed in the most
public manner. Rising in his box, between
the acts, my lord sent for Barton Booth, and
presented him with a purse of fifty guineas as
some acknowledgment for his "defending the
cause of liberty so well against a perpetual
dictator." This perpetual dictator being none
other than the great Duke of Marlborough, a
staunch Whig, who at this time sought the post
of Commander-in-chief for life.

All through the five acts of *Cato*, the excitement, applause, and noise never lagged.
The *Examiner*, speaking of this night, says
that Sir Gilbert, whom it irreverently terms
Sir Gilby, "and his band of little critics from
Change," gave their zeal an advantage over
their understanding, and applauded with much
awkward fury in the wrong parts;" whilst it
again refers to a "croud of silly people,
creatures wearing the ornaments of the head

altogether on the outside," who were "drawn up under the leadership of the renowned Ironside, and appointed to clap at his signals." The renowned Ironside being of course Dick Steele.

The while, Addison "sweated behind the scenes with concern," as Pope records. Uncertain of the manner in which his play would be received, and fearful of hazarding his brilliant reputation by a failure, he was filled by tremulous anxiety. His nervous concern would not permit him to remain away from the playhouse, nor yet allow him to sit as one of the audience. He therefore took himself behind the scenes, to await his fate with such patience as he could summon to his aid. "Placing himself on a bench in the greenroom," writes Mrs. Inchbald, "his body motionless, his soul in tumult, he kept by his side a friend, whom he despatched every minute towards the stage, to bring him news of what was passing there. He thus secured, he conceived, progressive information of his fate, without the risk of hearing it from an enraged multitude. But such was the vehemence of applause, that shouts of ad-

miration forced their way through the walls of
the greenroom, before his messenger could return
with the gladsome tidings. Yet not till the
last sentence was spoken, and the curtain fairly
dropped upon Cato and his weeping friends, did
the author venture to move from the inanimate
position in which he was fixed. The acute
dread of failure now heightened the joy of
success ; and never was success more complete."
The tragedy was acted for thirty nights to
enthusiastic audiences ; its run being chiefly due
to the political points of view from which it
was regarded, for as a play it was unsuited to
the requirements of the stage. Mrs. Inchbald
naïvely enough points out the cause which
hindered its permanent success. "With all its
patriotism it must ever," she writes, "be a dull
entertainment to the female sex ; and men of
course receive but little pleasure from elegant
amusements of which women do not partake."

No sooner had it run its course in London
than the tragedy was taken to Cambridge by the
managers of Drury Lane, that it might be presented to a widely different class of audience. The

flashy wit and broad humour which delighted the metropolitan crowd were here discountenanced. "Shakespeare and Ben Jonson had there a sort of classical authority," says Colley Cibber, "for whose masterly scenes they seemed to have as implicit a reverence as formerly for the ethics of Aristotle, and were as incapable of allowing moderns to be their competitors as of changing their academical habits for gaudy colours of embroidery." But to Addison, who had imbibed his classic lore within the stately walls of this Alma Mater, the students were most willing to give ear. The fame of the play had travelled far, and expectations almost as great as those which awaited its first representation at London were now entertained at Cambridge. Accordingly, on the day announced for its performance, the entrance to the theatre was besieged before noon; at twelve o'clock admission was no longer possible—the house was full. For three days, Cibber tells us, the same enthusiasm continued, "and," adds he, "the death of Cato triumphed over the enemies of Cæsar everywhere."

Towards the end of April the tragedy was
published by Jacob Tonson, "at Shakespeare's
Head, against Catherine Street, in the Strand,"
and in a short time as many as ten thousand
copies were sold.  Then came the first shadow
that crossed the brightness of its success.  This
was no bigger than a man's hand, and was in
truth a pamphlet from the pen of John Dennis,
a satirist by nature and critic by profession, who
passed, as he tells us, " for a man who was con-
ceitedly resolved to like nothing which others
like."  Though the play had been set before the
world for the advantage of the Whigs, and Dennis
was a hired flatterer in the interests of that party,
yet he could not, according to Johnson, "sit quiet
and see a successful play, but was eager to tell
his friends and enemies that they had misplaced
their admiration."

For this purpose he wrote a pamphlet, entitled,
" Remarks upon *Cato*," which was published by
Lintott, " at the Cross Keys, between the two
Temple Gates in Fleet Street."  Dennis prefaces
his criticism by stating that for weeks his friends
had urged him to make some remarks upon the

play, whose great success prognosticated ruin for the tragic stage. He was aware there had appeared numerous encomiums—nicknamed criticisms—on the piece, but these had, he presumed, been written by authors retained for the purpose, who, believing, like conscientious lawyers, it was their duty to say all they could for their client, had done their best to honestly earn their fees. Now, Mr. Dennis felt sure nothing but wholesome criticism could revive public taste; and therefore the errors and absurdities of *Cato* should be set in a true light by him, or the tragic muse must be banished from the island. This was the keynote of a tedious piece of criticism filling upwards of fifty quarto pages. The chief points of attack were that the conduct of Cato was replete with inconsistencies; that death by his own hand carried with it, not a moral lesson, but a pernicious instruction; and that as a drama it had neither the art nor the contrivance of an entertaining novel or an agreeable romance, by which curiosity is excited, longing provoked, agitation aroused, and satisfaction secured.

This pamphlet fell upon the town with startling

effect, but it by no means changed the popular current concerning a play which Johnson declared the noblest work of Addison's genius. The attack was, of course, unexpected, and bewildered its victim. But he was too wise a man in his generation to give public indication of his feelings, and therefore forbore defending himself by publishing a reply addressed to his critic, but intended for the tówn, as was the custom of authors and others smarting under abusive attacks. Dennis's criticism would have lost half its notoriety had this example been followed by others; but, alas, one of the irrepressible tribe who ever flock round notable men quickly scrambled into the arena, and in an undignified manner picked up the gauntlet which Addison had not deigned to notice.

This friend, none other indeed than Mr. Pope, was prompted to sturdy action by strong personal motives. It had happened this little poetical gentleman had some time before published an Essay on Criticism, in which he had stepped out of his way to pass certain strictures on John Dennis. Now a critic or satirist, as all the world knows, is an individual who will not permit others to indulge in those pleasant liberties with him which he delights in taking with them. John Dennis, being no exception to the general rule, first fell foul of the essay itself, and subsequently of Pope's Rape of the Lock. Highly impressible and fiercely malignant, the poet cherished in his diminutive person the sensitiveness of a woman and the instincts of a wasp. He had bided his time, and now came an opportunity which was golden ; for it permitted him, whilst aiming the bitterest arrows of his wrath at his enemy, to shelter himself behind the shield of his friendship for Addison.

Accordingly he rushed into print and published a pamphlet, now most rare, having of course no place in his published works. This effusion bore the following lengthy title : " The Narrative of Dr. Robert Norris, concerning the strange and deplorable frenzy of Mr. John Dennis. Being an exact account of all that past betwixt the said patient and the doctor till the present day ; and a full vindication of himself and his proceedings from the extravagant reports of the said Mr. John Dennis." Now Dr. Robert Norris was a veritable physician, living at the sign of the Pestle and Mortar on Snow Hill, who advertised in the *Flying Post and Daily Courier* he had "experience in the cure of lunatics, and hath conveniences and suitable attendance at his own house for either sex ; so that any person applying themselves as above may have unquestionable hope that the cure shall be speedily and industriously endeavoured, and (by God's blessing) effected on reasonable terms." That this excellent man fell foul of Mr. Pope for using his name, history does not say.

The writer of the pamphlet narrates that as he was pondering in his closet one day over the case of a patient, he heard a knocking at the door, opening which there entered an old woman, who with tears in her eyes declared without his assistance her master would be utterly ruined. On inquiring who this gentleman might be, she told him it was Mr. John Dennis ; and being furthermore questioned, revealed the facts that since April he had been taken ill of a violent frenzy, and had since continued in those melancholy circumstances with few or no intervals. His extravagancies had been brought about in the simplest manner, in no other way indeed than by the receipt of a book, after reading which he stared "ghastfully," raved aloud, and muttered the word Cator or Cato. On hearing these strange tidings the doctor, taking up his cane and beaver, repaired to the lodgings where the afflicted patient lived, situated near Charing Cross, and reached by three pair of stairs. Here Dr. Norris found the unfortunate gentleman seated on his bed, with Lintott the bookseller on one side of him, and on the other a grave-looking gentleman, "the latitude of whose countenance was not a little eclipsed by the fullness of his peruke." As for the patient, "his aspect was furious; his eyes, which he rolled about in an uncommon manner, were rather fiery than lively. He often opened his mouth as if he would have uttered some matters of importance, but the sound seemed

F

lost inwardly; his beard was grown, which he would not suffer to have shaved, believing the modern dramatic poets had corrupted all barbers in town to take the first opportunity of cutting his throat; his eyebrows were gray, long, and grown together, which he knit with indignation when anything was spoken, insomuch that he seemed not to have smoothed his forehead for many years. His flannel night-cap, which was exceedingly begrimed with sweat and dirt, hung upon his left ear, and the rolls of his stockings fell down upon his ankles."

Then followed some details concerning his room: " on all sides of which were pinned a great many sheets of a tragedy called *Cato,* with notes on the margin with his own hand; the words absurd, monstrous, execrable, being written in such large characters," says Dr. Norris, "that I could read them without my spectacles." Presently the afflicted Mr. Dennis began to rave.

" Alas! what is to become of the drama ?" says he.

" The dram, sir," says the old woman, who

had summoned the doctor; "Mr. Lintott drank up all the Geneva just now, but I'll fetch more presently."

"O shameful want," says Dennis. "By all the immortals here is no *peripartia*, no change of fortune in the tragedy. Zounds, no change at all."

"Pray, good sir," chimes in the old woman soothingly, "be not angry, I'll fetch change."

After pages of such dialogue the unfortunate gentleman was bound hand and foot to the bed, whereon he grew so violent the doctor and Mr. Lintott had to leave the room in all expedition imaginable.

Now Addison, recognising Pope's motives, by no means appreciated the pamphlet, which merely attacked Dennis in a scurrilous manner, whilst leaving the criticisms on *Cato* wholly untouched. It was at once beneath Addison's dignity to approve of this retort or appear to connive at its pettiness, facts which he was anxious to have conveyed to Dennis. Accordingly, he employed his friend Steele to pen a brief note to Lintott. "Mr. Addison desired me to tell you," writes Steele to the publisher, "he wholly disapproves of the manner of treating Mr. Dennis in a little pamphlet by way of Dr. Norris's account. When he thinks fit to take notice of Mr. Dennis's objections to his writings, he will do it in a way that Mr. Dennis shall have no just reason to complain of; but when the papers above mentioned were communicated to him, he said he could not either in honour or conscience be privy to such a treatment, and was sorry to hear of it!"

Pope, however, had no desire to be ignored by the great Mr. Addison, and accordingly sent him an epistle, clearly to excuse his raillery, and ingratiate himself in Addison's favour; the letter is moreover eminently characteristic of its ingenuous writer. "I am more joy'd at your return," it begins, "than I should be at that of the sun, so much as I wish for him this melancholy wet season; but 'tis his fate too, like yours, to be displeasing to owls, and obscure animals, who cannot bear his lustre. What put me in mind of these night-birds was John Dennis, whom I think you are best revenged upon, as the sun was in the fable, upon those bats and beastly birds above mentioned, only by shining on." He then proceeds to state he is far from esteeming it a misfortune, and rather congratulates his friend upon having his share in that which all great and good men that ever lived have had their part of, envy and malice. " To be uncensured," he continues, " and to be obscure is the same thing. You may conclude from what I here say, that 'twas never in my thoughts to have offered you my pen on any direct reply to such a critic, but only in some little raillery; not in defence of you, but in contempt of him. But indeed your opinion that 'tis to be entirely neglected, would have been my own had it been my own case; but I felt more warmth here than I did when first I saw his book against myself (tho' indeed in two minutes it made me heartily merry). He has written against everything the world has approved these many years. I apprehend but one danger from Dennis's dis-

G

liking our sense, that it may make us think so
very well of it, as to become proud and conceited
upon his disapprobation."

This letter, which ends the story of Addison's
tragedy, had not the desired effect, and a cool-
ness soon sprang up between Addison and Pope
which lasted many years.

# JOHN GAY'S BEGGAR'S OPERA.

FIRST PRODUCED, 29TH JANUARY, 1728.

George II. Ascends the Throne—The New King's House-
hold—John Gay Seeks a Profitable Place—Offer of an
Ushership—Disappointment and Chagrin—Suggestion
of *The Beggar's Opera*—Congreve Gives His Opinion—
Political Allusions—First Production of the Opera—
Immediate Success—Gay's Second Opera—Quarrels at
Court—Gay's Fortune Secured.

G 2

# JOHN GAY'S BEGGAR'S OPERA.

ON the afternoon of the 12th day of June, in the year of grace 1727, Sir Robert Walpole, then Prime Minister of England, rode in hot haste to Richmond that he might inform the Prince of Wales, George I. had died suddenly at Osnaburg. History narrates that, roused from his customary nap which an early and over-hearty dinner was wont to induce, the new monarch tumbled out of bed, and rushed into the antechamber breeches in hand, where he found the great minister on his knees waiting to hail him king. Next day the silent and expectant multitudes thronging the streets of London town were duly informed that, by the grace of God, George Augustus Guelph had succeeded to the throne of Great Britain and Ireland as George II.

The sudden death of the late king, and the proclamation of the new, caused a prodigious sensation among statesmen, courtiers, and place-hunters. The favourites of his late majesty were heavy at heart, knowing their day of triumph had passed for ever; the followers of the present monarch were filled with joy, believing their hour of exaltation at hand. The court end of the town presented a scene of vast excitement. By night and by day the state-rooms of Leicester House, situated in Leicester Square, where the Prince and Princess had lived since their banishment from St. James's, and to which they now returned from Richmond, were thronged by most loyal crowds anxious to kiss their majesties' hands. The square outside presented an unusually brilliant spectacle which, phantasmagoria-like, changed continually, without loss of colour and with gain of variety; for here were gathered together courtiers, politicians, gossips, soldiers, citizens, players, poets, pamphleteers, coachmen, chairmen, and footmen, all busy with unquiet speculation regarding what alteration in the affairs of state this new reign would produce.

Now, amongst those who looked forward with impatient anxiety to a profitable place in their majesties' household, was John Gay the poet. He was a man who in his time had played many parts, and had for upwards of fourteen years posed as a courtier in the drawing-rooms of the present sovereigns when Prince and Princess of Wales. Born of an ancient and worthy Derbyshire family, he had been bred a mercer; had served the imperious Duchess of Monmouth as secretary; and had travelled into Holland with my Lord Clarendon in a like capacity. Returning to England with his lordship on the accession of George I., he had written a poem regarding the new Princess of Wales, describing her to the English ladies before she came over. This effusion, under the guise of loyal homage, shaped itself to a courteous petition for place; it resulted in procuring him the favour of her he addressed without gaining him the reward he expected. However, he became regular in his attendance at court, and subsequently formed one of that gay and gracious assembly of wits, gallants, and beauties which gave a character for brilliancy, politeness, and pleasure to the drawing-rooms of Leicester House, such as had been unknown to the English court since the days of the Merry Monarch.

Here the blond and stately Princess was surrounded by her fair maids of honour, foremost amongst whom were the piquant Mary Bellenden and the charming Molly Lepel, both possessing a reputation for winsomeness and beauty. Here also assembled such notable figures as my Lord Chesterfield, wittiest of wits, most courteous of courtiers; Lord John Hervey, surnamed the "handsome," a superfine gentleman, daintily rouged, elegantly ruffled, and delicately perfumed; the Duchess of Queensberry, eccentric in speech and dress; the mad Duchess of Buckingham, who hatched foolish plots for the exiled Stuarts' return; Dean Swift, who made sharp speeches to the Princess; Lady Mary Wortley Montagu, who engaged the amorous attentions of the Prince; and young Colonel Campbell, then secretly married to Mary Bellenden, whom he afterwards raised to be Duchess of Argyle.

Notwithstanding his constant attendance at

court, and his loyal homage to the Princess, Gay remained unrewarded.

"I have been considering," writes Dean Swift to him, "why poets have such ill success in making their court, since they are allowed to be the greatest and best of all flatterers. The defect is that they flatter only in print or in writing, but not by word of mouth. They will give things under their hand which they make a conscience of speaking. Besides, they are too libertine to haunt antechambers, too poor to bribe porters and footmen, and too proud to cringe to second-hand favourites in a great family."

Gay's attendance at court was actuated by constant expectation of reward ; but whilst hope sustained his poetic soul, it entirely failed to nourish his corpulent body or enable him to dress in "silver loops and garments blue," in accordance with his vain desires.

That he might live he therefore wooed the Muses, and wrote poems and plays which had more or less success : more where his poems—the subscription for which realised him one thousand pounds—were concerned ; less with regard to

his plays. One of thése, *The Wife of Bath*,
was damned at its birth; whilst his burlesque
farce, *What D'ye Call It*, and his tragedy, *The
Captives*, were short-lived, though patronised by
royalty.

Some of his friends in office had, however,
proved kind, and in 1723 he had been appointed
Commissioner of the State Lottery, a post he
held for two years, and then lost at the instance
of Sir Robert Walpole, who believed him to have
written a pamphlet dealing severely with government measures.

Now the Prince and Princess had come to the
throne, Gay's hopes revived. In order to keep
his memory green in the hearts of royalty, he
had written a book of very ingenious fables in
verse for the amusement and instruction of Prince
William, afterwards known to his generation as
"Billy the Butcher;" and, in reference to the story
of the " Hare and Many Friends," the Princess
told Mrs. Howard, her bed-chamber woman,
she would take up the hare, and requested
she would put her in mind of Mr. Gay when the
household came to be. settled. Hearing of this

gracious speech, John Gay believed himself on the broad road to certain honour and high reward.

Endowed with the poetic temperament, his moods of hope and dejection followed each other as regularly as light and shadow on April days; and now his expectations were at their meridian. Perhaps it was his sanguine disposition, together with a certain simplicity of character, which enabled him to make his way quickly to the hearts of all with whom he came in contact. Pope, having "seen too much of his good qualities to be anything less than his friend," described him to Spence as "quite a natural man, wholly without art or design, who spoke just what he thought, and as he thought it;" and Swift, who loved him likewise, gave it as his opinion Providence never intended the poet "to be above two-and-twenty by his thoughtlessness and gullibility."

The royal household in due time was settled, and Gay, after fourteen long years' attendance at court, "with a large stock of real merit, a modest and agreeable conversation, a hundred promises, and five hundred friends," was offered the post of usher to the Princess Louisa, who had then reached the mature age of ten years. Though this post was worth two hundred a year, Gay rejected it with indignation, abandoned St. James's, and forswore courtly servility for evermore. " The Queen's family is at last settled," he writes to Dean Swift, then in Ireland, " and in the list I was appointed Gentleman Usher to the Princess Louisa, the youngest princess ; which, upon account that I am so far advanced in life, I have declined accepting. So now all my expectations have vanished, and I have no prospect but in depending wholly upon myself and my own conduct. As I am used to disappointments I can bear them ; but as I can have no more hopes, can no more be disappointed, so that I am in a blessed condition." The poor dean had likewise suffered many sore vexations at the hands of statesmen and courtiers such as Gay now endured ; and was quick to sympathise with him. Swift therefore wrote back he entirely approved of Gay refusing the appointment, and by way of comforting the poet, hoped he might soon obtain

some other situation which "will be better cir-
cumstantiated."

Pope likewise sought to soothe Gay's chagrin,
and reminded him he had often repeated a ninth
beatitude for his benefit: "Blessed is he who
expects nothing, for he shall never be disappointed." Instead of feeling regret, he continues,
he could find it in his heart to congratulate him
on a happy dismissal from all court dependence.
"I dare say," he adds, "I shall find you the
better and the honester man for it many years
hence; very probable the healthfuller and the
cheerfuller into the bargain. You are happily
rid of many cursed ceremonies as well as of many
ill and vicious habits, of which few or no men
escape the infection who are hackneyed or tram-
melled in the ways of a court. Princes indeed,
and peers, the lackies of princes, and ladies, the
fools of peers, will smile on you the less, but
men of worth and real friends will look on you
the better."

Gay's depression was not of long continuance,
for it happened he had at this critical time just
finished his *Beggar's Opera*, which was soon destined

to create a considerable sensation throughout the kingdom. Eleven years previously, a hint, serving as the germ for this opera, had been conveyed to him in a letter Swift wrote Pope. There was a young, ingenious Quaker living in Dublin who penned verses to his mistress, "not very correct, but in a strain purely what a poetical Quaker should do, commending her look and habit." This caused Swift to think a set of Quaker pastorals might succeed, and he asks Pope to hear what their friend Gay says on the subject. "I believe farther," he continues, "the pastoral ridicule is not exhausted, and that a porter, footman, or chairman's pastoral might do well. Or what think you of a Newgate pastoral amongst the thieves?" Later on, as we learn from Pope, Swift said to Gay, "What an odd pretty sort of thing a Newgate pastoral might make!"

Gay was inclined to think a comedy having scenes laid in the famous prison might be better still, and hence the origin of *The Beggar's Opera.* "He began on it," says Pope, "and, when first he mentioned it to Swift, the doctor did not much like the project. As he carried it on he showed what he wrote to both of us; and we now and then gave a correction, or a word or two of advice, but it was wholly of his own writing. When it was done, neither of us thought it would succeed. We showed it to Congreve, who, after reading it over, said, 'It would either take greatly, or be damned confoundedly!'"

Gay attributed his bitter disappointment, on being offered an ushership to a royal baby, not to the queen, but rather to Sir Robert Walpole, who had previously ousted him from his commissioner-ship. In this opinion he was strengthened by Swift, who hinted Sir Robert was his keen enemy, whereon the pious dean prayed God to forgive him; "but not," says he, in safe reservation, "until he puts himself in a state to be forgiven." Feeling grievously injured, Gay accordingly de-termined to avenge his wrongs on courtiers and ministers in general, and the Prime Minister in particular. Therefore, though his opera was finished, he skilfully changed it so as to compare, as Swift says, "the common robbers of the public, and their several stratagems of betraying, under-

mining, and hanging each other, to the several
arts of the politicians in times of corruption."
Moreover, he pointed his dialogue sufficiently to
sting the man he considered his enemy; added
verses satirising the court; and introduced a
scene in which two notorious rascals, Lockit and
Peachum, wrangle, in commemoration of a similar
quarrel which a little while before had taken
place in public between Walpole and Pulteney.
Time has, of course, served to blunt many of the
speeches of their original sharpness, but we can
well imagine how such sentences as that in which
Peachum tells Lockit their employment as go-
betweens for thieves "may be reckoned dishonest
because, like great statesmen, we encourage those
who betray our friends," must have galled the
men for whom they were intended.

When *The Beggar's Opera* was quite finished
it was offered to Colley Cibber and his brother
managers of Drury Lane, who promptly rejected it; whereon it was carried to John Rich,
at this time proprietor of Lincoln's Inn Fields
Theatre. Rich accepted the play, speedily put
it in rehearsal, and on the 29th of January, 1728,

printed the following announcement in the *Daily Post :*

Never Before Acted
By the Company of Comedians
At the Theatre Royal in Lincoln's Inn Fields.
The present Monday being the 29th day of January, will be
Performed
THE BEGGAR'S OPERA.
Boxes, 5s.; Pit, 3s.; Gallery, 2s.

On the night of its first representation Gay's many friends assembled at the old playhouse in the Fields; being much concerned for the success of his opera, and determined to give it what support they could. Moreover a vast crowd of women of quality and men of parts was present, whom curiosity or the hope of diversion had drawn to this end of the town. The piece commended itself in the strongest manner to popular taste, inasmuch as according to rumour it sparkled with wit slightly screening innuendo, and ridiculed morality in the freest manner. On the other hand a ballad opera was a form of entertainment new to the public, and it was impossible to know how it might be received. Pope tells us he and Gay's friends were in great uncertainty at its first pro-

H

duction, "till," says he, "we were very much encouraged by overhearing the Duke of Argyle, who sat in the next box to us, saying, 'It will do—it must do ; I see it in the eyes of them.' This was a good while before the first act was over, and so gave us ease soon. For the duke, besides his own good taste, has a more particular knack than any one now living in discovering the taste of the public. He was quite right in this as usual ; the good-nature of the audience appeared stronger and stronger every act, and ended in a clamour of applause."

Its success was assured before the curtain fell, and the acclamations which rang through the house were said to be "the greatest ever known." The sensation it created elicited a criticism from the *Daily Journal* two days later, a most rare occurrence and certain sign of distinction in those days. "On Monday," this notice says, "was represented for the first time at the Theatre Royal in Lincoln's Inn Fields, Mr. Gay's English opera, written in a manner wholly new, and very entertaining, there being introduced, instead of Italian airs, above sixty of the most celebrated old English and

Scotch tunes. There was present then, as well as last night, a prodigious concourse of nobility and gentry; and no theatrical performance for these many years has met with so much applause."

The excitement it caused throughout the length and breadth of London was indeed remarkable. The exterior of Lincoln's Inn Fields playhouse nightly presented a scene of confusion. Crowds blocked the doors hours previous to their opening; linkboys, chairmen, and footmen wrangled to make place for their masters and employers; orange-women cried their wares in shrill tones; ballad singers droned and sold songs of the opera; sedans jostled each other amidst the curses of Hibernian carriers; and the constant and heavy roll of ponderous coaches added to the general noise and bustle. Inside the theatre, men of all parties and women of every condition assembled; ministers who were ridiculed came to protest their indifference to satire by laughing with the crowd; and grave clergymen, doffing their bands and gowns, sat disguised in the pit amongst saucy coxcombs.

For sixty-three consecutive nights *The Beggar's*

*Opera* was performed in the season, a rare distinction in times when three nights was the
average run of a play. Nor was this all. It
drove the Italian opera, which it burlesqued,
out of town; its songs were sung in every
drawing-room; and its verses printed on the
fans of women of quality. Its fame spread from
the capital all over the kingdom, it was played
in the larger towns in England, and finally
made its way to Scotland, Wales, and Ireland.

"We are as full of it," writes Dean Swift,
writing from Dublin to the successful author, "'pro
modulo nostro,' as London can be; continually
acting, and houses crammed, and the Lord Lieutenant several times there, laughing his heart
out. We hear a million of stories about the
opera, of the applause of the song when two
great ministers were in a box together, and all
the world staring at them."

No doubt portion of the success was due to
the vivacious and witty manner in which the
characters of the hero and heroine were played
by Walker, and Lavinia Fenton. At first, the
part of Captain Macheath was offered by the

author to James Quin, who had, as Davies tells us, "so happy an ear for music, and was so famous for singing with ease a common ballad or catch;" but after a short trial at rehearsal Quin gave it up, "from despair of acquitting himself with the dissolute gaiety and bold vigour of deportment necessary to the character." It was then offered to Walker, who, though he had but an indifferent voice and could barely sing in tune, acted with so much drollery that he gave entire satisfaction to author and audience alike.

In the character of the heroine, Polly Peachum, Miss Fenton gained both fame and fortune, as will hereafter be narrated. Up to this time she had in no way raised herself above her theatrical contemporaries, and was merely noted as an actress possessing a vivacious spirit and a fascinating beauty, both of which she had freely exhibited on the stage of Lincoln's Inn Fields Theatre, for the sum of fifteen shillings weekly. But the part of Polly Peachum affording full scope for her talents, her innate grace, her winning archness, and seductive ways, greatly delighted the town and caused Rich to double her salary.

The story of her life of twenty summers was calculated to heighten the interest her perform-ance inspired. The daughter of a gay young naval officer, named Beswick, she had come into the world in the year 1708, whilst he was sailing on the seas. Soon after, her mother, yearning for congenial companionship, married one Fenton in the Old Bailey; but being "a woman of a popular spirit," she soon established a coffee-house near Charing Cross. Here her little daughter Lavinia, a vivacious child, became a favourite of certain fops, who taught her snatches of such play-house songs as was the pleasure of these pretty gentlemen to hum, whilst sipping their coffee or making love to her mamma. To this coffee-house came likewise an actor from the old house, who, hearing her sing, took some interest in giving her instructions in music, and she being apt, her rapid progress repaid him for his pains.

In the next chapter of her life we find Miss Fenton at a boarding-school, where she was ad-mired by a gallant spark from the Inner Temple, who, by bribing a porter, gained admittance to the garden surrounding this polite academy for

young ladies. Here he pledged vows of eternal
love to his adored Lavinia. This, however, was
but a school-girl's romance ; indeed but a mere
prelude to episodes of the same interesting complexion; for, on leaving the academy, she fell
in love with a wealthy Portuguese nobleman.
This lover behaved so liberally to her that he was
soon carried to the Fleet prison ; from which scene
of durance vile grateful Lavinia, by the sale of
her jewels, was enabled to release him. Soon
after, in 1726, being now in her eighteenth
year, she found her way through the stage door
of the new Haymarket Theatre, then under the
management of Huddy. Here she made her
curtsy to the town, which received her with considerable applause ; for having, as a contemporary
critic said, "a lively imagination, joined with a
good memory, a clear voice, and a graceful mien,
she seemed as if nature had designed her for the
pleasure of mankind in such performances as are
exhibited at our theatre !"

The great triumph of her career was, however,
reserved for her appearance in *The Beggar's Opera,*
in which she was pronounced inimitable. Her

gray eyes sparkling with merriment, her softly
rounded cheeks suffused with blushes, her cherry
lips parted in smiles, her graceful form bending to
a curtsy, she came forward night after night to
receive universal applause. When enthusiasm
had subsided, and she had spoken the first lines
of her part declaring a woman knew how to be
mercenary, though she had never been in a court
or at an assembly, she broke into the song,
"Virgins are like the fair flow'r in its lustre,"
and by her piquancy completed the fascination
her appearance had begun. Her name was on
all men's lips; her pictures were engraved and
sold in great numbers; books of letters and
verses addressed to her were published, and
pamphlets made of her sayings and jests.

Amongst those who sat nightly in one of the
stage boxes at Lincoln's Inn playhouse, was
Charles Powlett, third Duke of Bolton, then in
his forty-third year. His grace was a man of
pleasure well known to the town, and was moreover, as Swift assures us, "a great booby, who
does not make any figure at court, or anywhere
else." He had, fifteen years before, married the

daughter and sole heiress of the Earl of Carberry,
with whom he had never lived; and he now found
himself desperately in love with Lavinia Fenton,
who was nothing loth to receive his homage or
accept his settlement of four hundred a year
during his pleasure, and half that amount upon
their separation.

Accordingly when, on the 19th of June, in
this year, *The Beggar's Opera* was played for the
last time during this season, Mistress Fenton
made her farewell bow to the public as an actress.
So accomplished and agreeable a companion did
the duke find her, so well did her wit, sense, and
tact delight him, that she retained his affections
during the remainder of his life, a space covering
some five-and-twenty years. She bore him three
sons, and, on the death of his duchess in 1751,
he raised Lavinia to the peerage. He survived
this act but three years. The new duchess lived
on for six years more, not wholly uncomforted
for his loss; for, being at Tunbridge, as we read
in Horace Walpole's Letters, "she picked up an
Irish surgeon," to whom, as a memento of their
mutual happiness, she bequeathed when dying,

the sum of nine thousand pounds; to her three sons she left one thousand pounds each.

By-and-by *The Beggar's Opera* was published, and then, as if to keep its memory fresh, a hot dispute arose regarding its effect on public morals. Swift gave it as his conviction that Gay, "by a turn of humour entirely new, placed vices of all kinds in the strongest and most odious light, and thereby had done eminent service both to religion and morality." The Rev. Thomas Herring, a court chaplain, who afterwards became Arch-bishop of Canterbury, entirely differed from the dean in his opinion, and even ventured to denounce the opera from the pulpit. Whereon the Irish parson waxed exceeding wroth, and gave vent to his hopes in the third number of the *Intelligencer*, that "no clergyman should be so weak as to imitate a court chaplain who preached against *The Beggar's Opera*, which will probably do more good than a thousand sermons of so stupid, so injudicious, a divine." The argument did not end here; for that worthy justice, Sir John Fielding, declared "many robbers had confessed they had been seduced by *The Beggar's*

*Opera* to begin the commission of those crimes which finally brought them to the gallows."

The great success of the piece inclined John Gay to write another in the same style, brief mention of which will serve, as an epilogue to *The Beggar's Opera*. Accordingly, next year a second ballad opera entitled *Polly*, sequel to the first, was ready for the stage, and great were the expectations it raised throughout the town. But the poet counted without his host; for the ministry, being secretly enraged by the plentiful satire contained in the former entertainment, declined to brook further ridicule from the same pen, and ordered the Lord Chamberlain — his Grace of Grafton—to suppress the new piece. This was regarded by Gay and his admirers as an act of revenge; for the second opera was more decent in its language, and more respectful in its tone to those in high places, than its predecessor. The prohibition was issued without any charge being made against a part or parts of the piece; but later on Gay says he was accused in general terms of having written many disaffected libels, seditious pamphlets, and

immoralities, and was informed that his new
opera was "filled with slanders and calumnies
against particular great persons, and that majesty
itself was endeavoured to be brought into ridicule, and contempt," of all which dreadful charges
he avows himself most innocent in thought,
word, and action.

There was yet, however, one card in this
game between himself and the ministry left for
him to play. Though the public might not see
his opera on the stage there was no law to
prevent them reading its pages at home, and
accordingly it was sent to press. This was
better for Gay, from a pecuniary point of view,
than if his piece had been duly produced. For,
lacking the wit and humour his late opera
contained, it would probably not have obtained
similar success on the boards, whilst in its
published form it was, as the composition of
one persecuted by the ministry and neglected by
royalty, rapidly subscribed for by a large section
of the community then in opposition alike to
court and government. Prominent amongst these
were the Duchess of Marlborough, who pre-

sented him with one hundred pounds for a single copy; Lord and Lady Essex, who gave him many proofs of their interest; and the Duchess of Queensberry, who warmly espoused his cause, liberally subscribed for his work, and carried him to live at the ducal residence in Burlington Gardens. Nay, her grace's enthusiasm on his behalf went still further, for, at one of the drawing-rooms at St. James's, she besought the courtiers to subscribe for the opera so obnoxious to royalty. It happened whilst she was engaged in this manner His Majesty entered the room, and, noticing how earnestly she conversed with some officers of the household, inquired the subject of her discourse. Hearing this question her grace answered boldly: "What must be agreeable to any one so humane as your Majesty, for it is an act of charity, and one to which I do not despair of bringing your Majesty to contribute."

The king at once understood to what the duchess referred; his face grew crimson with indignation, but he uttered no reply. However, when the drawing-room was over one of the vice-chamberlains was despatched to the duchess, with a verbal message from royalty forbidding her presence at court in future. Her grace was a woman of spirit, as was shown by the fact that no sooner had she received this command than, "for fear of mistakes," as she said, she immediately penned the following curious epistle, which she bade the vice-chamberlain carry to their majesties without delay:

"The Duchess of Queensberry," wrote she, "is surprised and well pleased that the king hath given her so agreeable a command as to stay from court, where she never came for diversion, but to bestow a great civility on the king and queen; she hopes by such an unprecedented order as this that the king will see as few as he wishes at his court, particularly such as dare to think or speak truth. I dare not do otherwise, nor ought not, nor could have imagined that it would not have been the very highest compliment that I could possibly pay the king to endeavour to support truth and innocence in his house, particularly when the

king and queen hath both told me that they
had not read Mr. Gay's play. I have certainly
done right then to stand by my own word,
rather than his Grace of Grafton's, who has
neither made use of truth, judgment, nor honour
through the whole affair, either for himself or
his friends."

Her grace, therefore, became an absentee from
St. James's.

Nor did the quarrel end here, for the Duke
of Queensberry, much against His Majesty's
desire, resigned his post as High Admiral of
Scotland, and was seen no more at court for
many a day. The noise created by the affair only
served to increase the fame of this new opera
and its author. "The inoffensive John Gay,"
writes Arbuthnot to Swift in a jocular vein,
"is now become one of the obstructions to the
peace of Europe, the terror of ministers, the
chief author of all the seditious pamphlets which
have been published against the government. He
has got several turned out of their places ; the
greatest ornament of the court banished from it

for his sake; another great lady in danger of being *chassée* likewise; about seven or eight duchesses pushing forward, like ancient circum-celliones * in the church, who shall suffer martyr-dom upon his account first. He is the darling of the city, and if he should travel about the country he would have hecatombs of roasted oxen sacrificed to him."

The happy result was, John Gay made over twelve hundred pounds by the sale of his opera, and gained the permanent friendship and pro-tection of the Duke and Duchess of Queensberry, with whom he lived for the remainder of his days.

---

* A sect of African heretics smitten with the desire of being martyrs.

# DR. JOHNSON'S IRENE.

FIRST PRODUCED, 6TH FEBRUARY, 1749.

Dr. Johnson Comes to Town—Life in the Great City—
Writing his Tragedy at Greenwich—David Garrick
Becomes Patentee of Drury Lane Theatre—Johnson's
Abuse and Jealousy—*Irene* Submitted to the Manager
—Anger and Alteration—The Tragedy Produced—
Aaron Hill's Description—In the Pit—Receipts of the
House.

# DR. JOHNSON'S IRENE.

IN the thirty-seventh year of the last century, Samuel Johnson had determined on seeking his fortune in London town—"the great field of genius and exertion," as Boswell terms it, "where talents of every kind have the fullest scope and fullest encouragement." The future lexicographer, then in his twenty-seventh year, was considered a scholar of ability, a philosopher in embryo, and a dramatic poet, whose verse had filled his friend Mr. Walmesley with hope "he would turn out a fine tragedy writer" some day. Sharing the opinion expressed by his patron, Johnson regarded a play he had composed as a means certain of securing him fame and fortune. It was named *Irene*, and took the form of tragedy. Its first lines had been written

I 2

whilst he kept the famous school at Edial, where "were taught the Latin and Greek languages by Samuel Johnson," to young gentlemen whose domestic comforts fell to the charge of Mrs. Tetsy Johnson, a lady gifted by nature with "a bosom of more than ordinary protuberance." The tragedy was, however, completed elsewhere, for after a struggling existence of eighteen months the school dissolved, and the pupils who had so often gathered in tittering groups outside their master's bedroom door, that they might witness through the keyhole his "tumultuous and awkward fondness for Mrs. Johnson," were despatched to their various homes. Being free to face the world, Johnson turned his steps towards the great capital, carrying in his pockets the unfinished manuscript of his precious tragedy, and the sum of twopence-halfpenny. He was accompanied on his journey by one of his pupils, young David Garrick, who, years hence, was destined to produce the play at Drury Lane.

For some time after his arrival in London, few lines were added to the tragedy. The world knows how he existed during the first months of his sojourn in the great city — how he lodged with the staymaker Norris; breakfasted on bread and milk; dined for eightpence a day in excellent company at the Pine Apple, in New Street; spent hours in coffee-houses, listening to political discourses; visited only on clean-shirt days; went supperless to bed; and when lacking the pitiful means to secure rest and shelter, wandering through lonely streets and silent squares all night, till with the light of a new dawn fresh hopes arose in his breast.

But better days were at hand, and presently Johnson removed to Greenwich, where he took up his abode next door to the Golden Heart, in Church Street. And it being his pleasure to frequent the park through the fair summer months of this year 1737, his awkward figure—dressed in rusty brown, his knee-strings untied, his coat smeared with snuff, his head covered by a scratch wig and three-cornered hat—might be seen strutting to and fro where the fine old trees cast dreamy shadows on the grass. Walking here, he composed the last acts of his tragedy, which, with

characteristic appreciation of his work, he
considered destined to bear his name down
the stream of time to the envied haven of
fame.

But even the freedom and repose the park
afforded did not enable him to complete his
tragedy, and it was only when, towards the close
of summer, he returned to his native Lichfield
and his affectionate Tetsy the desired consum-
mation was obtained. The last line added, he
became impatient to reach town, and, after an
absence of three months, his familiar figure was
again seen taking its slow way to the Fountain
Tavern, in Fleet Street, that he might read his
tragedy to Peter Garrick. He next besought
Charles Fleetwood, the patentee of Drury Lane
playhouse, to consider his tragedy ; but he, being
accustomed to receive innumerable manuscripts
for perusal, was not likely to heed the merits of
an unknown writer. Accordingly *Irene* was
returned to its author, and for eleven years the
manuscript was laid aside. It was, however,
brought to the notice of Cave, editor and pro-
rietor of the *Gentleman's Magazine*, who, four

years after its rejection by Fleetwood, wrote to
Dr. Birch, a prominent member of the Society
for the Encouragement of Learning, requesting
he might give it consideration. The society
had been established for the purpose of assisting
authors in printing expensive works, and existed
from 1735 to 1746, when, being heavily encumbered
by debt, it was dissolved.

During the year 1747 David Garrick, now a
famous actor, became one of the patentees of
Drury Lane Theatre. Fate had smiled more
kindly on the pupil than on the master, in whose
company he had travelled to London just ten
years earlier. In a lucky hour Garrick had
abandoned the wine trade for the playhouse,
and risen in popular favour with a rapidity and
brilliancy which had no precedent in theatrical
history. Discarding the monotonous drawl, the
pretentious strut, the unnatural rant, which
up to this period had been regarded as legitimate modes of expressing pathos, assuming
loftiness, or betraying passion, he had introduced a school of natural acting, taken the
town by storm, and won admiration from the

highest intelligences in the land. The last step raising him to the summit of power was his succession to the management of old Drury Lane.

Now it was well known to Johnson's circle he regarded all actors in general, and David Garrick in particular, with a fine sense of contempt, which found continual expression in epigrammatic phrases. "Players, sir," he would grumble, "I look on them as no better than creatures set upon tables and joint-stools, to make faces and produce laughter like dancing dogs." But for Garrick, whose talent Boswell declares Johnson rated low in comparison with his own, his choicest shafts were reserved. "His being outstripped by his pupil," adds the biographer, "in the race of immediate fame, as well as of fortune, probably made him feel some indignation, as thinking that whatever might be Garrick's merits in his art, the reward was too great when compared with what the most successful efforts of literary labour could attain." Davies, in his Life of Garrick, likewise bears witness of Johnson's envy, and adds he never knew any other man who had the honesty and courage to confess this failing. When the actor was praised in his presence, it was the author's habit to speak of him as "poor Davy," in tones such as friends are wont to use when expressing sympathy but implying contempt for each other. He admitted Garrick possessed some convivial pleasantry, but qualified his acknowledgment by adding, "'tis a futile fellow." Then he was of opinion his sometime pupil lived in more splendour than was suitable to a player, that his wit was acquired and not spontaneous, and there was not one of his sceneshifters who could not speak "To be or not to be!" better than their manager. The fact was, Johnson considered the great actor, as Sir Joshua Reynolds said, to be his own property, and would allow no man to praise or blame him in his presence. This truth Boswell discovered to his cost, on that most memorable occasion when the admiring Scotchman came face to face with the philosopher for the first time, in Davies' back-parlour.

"What do you think of Garrick?" said Johnson to the retired actor and worthy bookseller. "He has refused me an order for the play for Miss Williams, because he knows the house will be full, and that an order would be worth three shillings." "Oh, sir," says Boswell, eager to enter into conversation with the ingenious author, "I cannot think Mr. Garrick would grudge such a trifle to you." "Sir," replied Johnson, with a stern look, "I have known David Garrick longer than you have done ; and I know no right you have to talk to me on the subject." And for once Boswell was subdued.

However, there were occasions when the great lexicographer expressed his admiration for Garrick's good qualities; and by way of proving the friendship he entertained for him, and celebrating the opening night of Drury Lane Theatre under its new manager, he penned a prologue, which found such favour with the town that its repetition was frequently called for during the season. Presently, when Garrick was fairly settled in his new position, it seemed to Johnson the time had come when *Irene* might be given to the world. The manager, possessing due admiration for his master's genius, was willing the tragedy should be produced, and anxious to accomplish aught lying in his power towards furthering its success. Accordingly, the play was submitted to his perusal, when he quickly discovered it by no means lent itself to dramatic representation. With considerable care he therefore informed Johnson though his tragedy, "from the propriety of the sentiments, the richness of the language, and the general harmony of the whole conception," was entitled to admiration in the closet, it was unsuited to the stage. To these comments he added various hints regarding certain changes that might be made with a view to its representation.

At these remarks Johnson's wrath was stirred to its depths, his indignation rose to fury. He who had already chastened the spirit and chastised the flesh of an insolent bookseller by knocking him down with one of his own folios, was dictated to by a player, and that player, of all others, "poor Davy." He to whom the publishers had agreed to give fifteen hundred guineas for his dictionary, "who had penned a beautiful and instructive biography," had suggestions made him by his own pupil concerning the embodied labour of years

Such things were not to be endured with patience by flesh and blood. Therefore disputes arose which threatened to terminate their friendship, when Garrick besought the Rev. Dr. Taylor that he might soften Johnson's wrath and convince him certain alterations were necessary to the performance of the tragedy. At first Johnson would not listen to the reverend man. " Why, sir," said he, in fine scorn, " the fellow wants me to make Mahomet run mad, that he may have an opportunity of tossing his hands and kicking his heels." By degrees, however, the full tide of his indignation subsided, and some changes were made in the play.

The plot of this tragedy, now seldom read even by Johnsonian students, was taken from an episode narrated in Knolles' History of Turkey, to the effect that Mahomet the Sultan, on being reproved by his courtiers for devoting overmuch time in dalliance with a certain favourite named Irene, to the neglect of affairs of state, resolved to re-establish himself in their favour. For this pur-pose he gathered the chiefs of his council together, summoned Irene, drew his sabre, and beheaded her. On this groundwork Johnson built his tragedy, varying it slightly from the original, and adding fresh incidents intended to promote its horror. In the play, a certain Cali Bassa conspires with two Greeks against the Sultan's life. One of these, Demetrius, loves a lady of the seraglio named Aspasia, whom he determines to rescue. Cali Bassa is detected and condemned to the rack, and whilst suffering accuses Irene of taking part in the conspiracy, whereon the outraged Sultan orders her to be strangled, and discovers her innocence after her death. This plot, encumbered with stately language and heavy philosophy, drags its slow way through four weary acts. A few days previous to his death, Johnson, in destroying a quantity of papers, found amongst them the original draft of the play, which he gave his friend Bennet Langton. The latter presented it to George III., having first made a fair copy of it. In due time, when George IV. was forced by Lord Liverpool to abandon the design of selling his father's library to the Emperor of Russia for the sum of one hundred and eighty thousand pounds, and accept instead a handsome equivalent that it might be preserved to the nation, Johnson's manuscript and its fair copy passed into the possession of the trustees of the British Museum, where they may yet be seen.

The tragedy having been altered, the parts were cast, the principal characters being taken by Garrick and Barry, Mrs. Cibber and Mrs. Pritchard. During the first month of the year 1749, Johnson's burly figure was seen daily, strutting between his lodgings in Gough Square and Drury Lane Theatre, where the play was being rehearsed. The part of Mahomet was assigned to Barry, an Irish actor remarkable for the extraordinary beauty of his person and delightful sweetness of his voice. Garrick elected to play Demetrius, the beautiful Susanna Cibber represented Aspasia; and Mrs. Pritchard, a lady remarkable for her grace and dignity, portrayed the sufferings of the luckless Irene.

On the 6th of February, 1749, the Drury

Lane play-bills bore the following announcement :

Never Acted before
By His Majesty's Company of Comedians.
At the Theatre Royal in Drury Lane
This day will be presented a New Tragedy, call'd
MAHOMET AND IRENE.
The principal parts to be performed by Mr. Garrick,

Mr. Barry,             Mr. Blakes,
Mr. Berry,             Mr. Usher,
Mr. Havard,            Mr. King,
Mr. Sowdon,            Mr. Pritchard,
And Mrs. Cibber.

Boxes, 5s.; Pit, 3s. ; First Gallery, 2s.; Upper Gallery, 1s.
To begin exactly at six o'clock.
'Tis hop'd no Gentleman will take it ill, they can't be
admitted behind the scenes.

Accordingly, on this eventful evening there was much ado at the theatre, both before the curtain, where critics occupied the front rows of the pit, and behind, where Garrick paced from greenroom to stage, betraying the nervous impatience habitual to him on first representations. Presently, when the house was full, burly Johnson entered, gaily attired in an ample scarlet waistcoat trimmed with gold, and furthermore adorned by a gold-laced hat, which sat awkwardly on his great head.  Wearing such accessories to his wardrobe which he deemed befitted the appearance of a dramatic author, he took his place in a side box, the observed of all observers ; now nodding his head in approbation to the sentiments uttered by the player, and anon, as Dr. Burney tells us, seeming " dissatisfied with some of the speeches and conduct of the play, and, like La Fontaine, expressing his disapprobation aloud."

Dr. Adams, who was likewise present at the first representation of *Irene,* gives the following account of what took place : " Before the curtain drew up, there were catcalls and whistling, which alarmed Johnson's friends.  The prologue, which was written by himself in a manly strain, soothed the audience, and the play went off tolerably till it came to the conclusion, when Mrs. Pritchard, the heroine of the piece, was to be strangled upon the stage, and was to speak two lines with the bowstring round her neck.  The audience cried out, ' Murder, murder !'  She several times attempted to speak, but in vain.  At last she was obliged to go off the stage alive." Davies adds the strangling of Irene in view of the audience, suggested by Garrick, was not approved by some of the critics, and "the incident after the first night was removed to a greater distance."

But though great things were expected of this tragedy, it became evident to all who witnessed its first representation it was not destined to meet with success. As Garrick foresaw, it had too much of the scholar's lore, and too little of the dramatist's art ; and therefore, as Arthur Murphy admits, "the united powers of Garrick, Barry, Mrs. Cibber, and Mrs. Pritchard could not lift it into vogue." Aaron Hill, himself a tragedy-writer, in a letter worth rescuing from the dusty oblivion into which his works have passed, gossips to his dear friend Mallet and "his excellent lady" concerning *Irene*. "I was in town," says he, "at the anomalous Mr. Johnson's benefit, and found the play his proper representative, strong sense, ungraced by sweetness or decorum. Mr. Garrick made the most of a detach'd and almost independent character. He was elegantly dress'd, and charm'd me infinitely, by an unexampled

K

silent force of painted action, and by a peculiar *touchingness*, in cadency of voice, from exclamation, sinking into pensive lownesses, that both surpriz'd and interested! Mrs. Cibber too was beautifully dressed, and did the utmost justice to her part. But I was sorry to see Mahomet (in Mr. Barry) lose the influence of an attractive figure and degrade the awfulness of an imperious Sultan, the impressive menace of a martial conqueror, and the beseeching tenderness of an amorous sollicitor, by an unpointed restlessness of leaping levity, that neither carried weight to suit his dignity, nor struck out purpose to express his passions."

For a couple of weeks the tragedy continued to exercise the judgment of large audiences. Opinions for and against it were freely delivered by day and night in coffee-houses and taverns, then the chief resorts of critics, and published in pamphlets and papers.

One worthy man, writing anonymously to the *General Advertiser*, gives a quaint description of the playhouse during the performance of *Irene.* The various and inconsistent reports of the piece exciting his curiosity strongly, he went to witness its representation on the sixth night of its performance.

"I took my station in the centre of the pit," says this observer, "that I might hear the opinion of the critics before the curtain drew up. I had not been long seated before I heard a voice pronounce with a kind of pert assurance, 'Dear me, there is not one line in it worth hearing.' I turned about, and perceived the speaker to be a tall, well-dressed young man, with a round unthinking face, and that he finished his sentence by taking a pinch of snuff with an air of great importance. At that instant, a person on my right hand told his companion that the first three acts were very fine, but that the author had been scandalously negligent in the fourth and fifth, which he intended to write over again, and bring the play on the stage next winter. Upon this, I conceived some hopes of my approaching entertainment, and was glad to hear that the author was at least thought able to mend his performance by those who condemn it as defective. This gentleman, perceiving me to be attentive to what he delivered, asked me if I had seen *Irene* before; upon my answering in the negative, he told me with an air of confidence that if I had not come that night I should not have seen it at all, for that it would be performed no more, and he even doubted whether the players would be suffered to go on. He further told me that the hero of the piece was one Demetrius, who undertook the delivery of his country, from no other principle than the love of a woman who was a captive in the Turk's seraglio; that there was no change of fortune in the play; that the plot was too simple, and that the whole piece had no moral.

"This brought to my mind Mr. John Dennis's exclamations against *Cato*, as they are related by Dr. Norris, in his narrative of that gentleman's deplorable phrenzy. As I conceived no exalted idea of this critic's abilities, from his manner of expression, I still continued in the same uncertainty as to the merit of the piece; and soon after, observing something in the mien and deportment of a gentleman who sat before me which strongly prejudiced me in his favour,

I asked his opinion. He told me he had seen the play the third night, but that the house being greatly crowded his situation prevented him from hearing every speech distinctly, and from seeing the actors to advantage, but that he thought the dialogue was full of sublime and virtuous sentiments, and though he did not pretend to be a critical judge whether all the rules of the drama were preserved, yet he thought the piece had great merit, and could not deny himself the pleasure of seeing from a more commodious seat.

"The curtain now drew up, and in less than five minutes I was convinced that the critic whose sentiments I first heard, formed his judgment of good lines by rules very different from my own. The three first acts confirmed the opinion of the second observer, but the fourth and fifth made me strongly suspect that he had been misinformed concerning the author's intention of new writing them. The falsehood of his prediction that the play would be no more acted appeared by its being given out for Thursday. This was received with universal approbation, upon which I turned about, and he, perceiving me smile in his face, instantly sneaked from his seat, with a look that convinced me he had more modesty than I before thought consisted with his criticism. Upon the whole, I dare affirm that the judgment of posterity will concur with me in distinguishing *Irene* as the best tragedy which this age has produced."

After solemnly delivering himself of this opinion, the writer proceeds to inquire why the play has not been so favourably received as others which had less merit to recommend them. The answer, he declares, is easy. *Irene* was devoid of "the perpetration of complicated murders, the appearance of bloody ghosts, the rants of heroes, and the whining of lovers." But all who admired *Irene* paid a compliment to their own judgment; "and it is," he concludes, "with the utmost pleasure that I tell the world, in honour of the ladies of Great Britain, that I scarce ever saw so shining an assembly in the boxes. Their early approbation of a tragedy in which not only the words but the ideas are entirely chaste, a tragedy filled with noble sentiment and poetic beauty, is at once a proof of their delicacy and penetration."

*Irene* was performed for nine nights only. John Wilson Croker, in a note to Boswell's Life of Johnson, states it to have been acted from Monday, the 6th of February, to Monday, the 20th of February inclusive, in all thirteen nights. The fact is, however, the play was not acted on the Wednesday or Friday nights of the fortnight during which it ran, and that it ended its brief career of nine nights on Monday, the 20th of February.

In all ways connected with this play, Garrick behaved in the handsomest manner to Johnson. Not only was the tragedy played by the best actors and actresses, but it was what was then styled " new dressed," that is, had costumes suited to the characters and period of the play specially made, an occurrence by no means common in those days. These, according to Davies, were rich and magnificent. " The scenes were splendid and gay, such as were well adapted to the inside of a Turkish seraglio ; and the view of the gardens belonging to it was in the taste of Eastern elegance.'' No only did the manager, by the exertion of his great powers, strive to endow the tragedy with vitality, but when these failed he had recourse to the additional attractions of farce and dance, allurements by which he hoped to draw crowded houses.

On the seventh night of the performance of *Irene*, it was therefore announced the tragedy would be succeeded by an "entertainment of dancing, particularly the Scotch dance by Mr. Cooke and Madame Anne Auretti; to which, by desire, will be added a farce call'd *The Anatomist; or, The Sham Doctor.*" On the next night, *The Lying Valet* was substituted for *The Anatomist;* and on the ninth and last night, *The Virgin Unmasked* was played, a favourite farce of Kitty Clive's, in which the brilliant actress appeared in the character of Miss Lucy. Out of the nine nights of *Irene's* performance, three were devoted to Johnson's benefit; on which occasions it was advertised tickets could be had of Mr. Miller, in the Strand, and Mr. Dodsley, in Pall Mall, booksellers both; at the Half Moon Tavern, near Holborn Bars; of Mrs. Payne, at the White Hart, in Paternoster Row; and of Mr. Hobson, at the stage-door of Drury Lane, where places might be taken. Though the play was voted the dullest piece imaginable, yet Johnson's private friends and public admirers bought tickets and took places on the occasions of his benefit nights readily enough. The results were by no means unsatisfactory. The receipts given in Mr. Alexander Napier's new edition of Boswell's Life of Johnson, taken from a manuscript note found in a copy of Murphy's biography of the great lexicographer, are set down as follows:

| | | |
|---|---:|---:|
| Third night's receipts . £177 | 1 | 6 |
| Sixth    „     „     . 106 | 4 | 0 |
| Ninth    „     „     . 101 | 11 | 6 |
| 384 | 17 | 0 |
| Charges of the House    . 189 | 0 | 0 |
| 195 | 17 | 0 |
| He also received for the copy 100 | 0 | 0 |
| In all    .    . £295 | 17 | 0 |

Since the 20th of February, 1749, the tragedy of *Irene* has never been acted. Johnson met his ill success as a playwright with philosophy, and never again attempted a dramatic work. When, years afterwards, he was asked how he felt regarding this comparative failure, he answered "Like the Monument;" meaning, as Boswell adds, "that he continued firm and unmoved as that column." He refrained, the same biographer tells us, from complaining, and gave it as his opinion the public to whom one appeals must after all be the judges of his pretensions.

So he cheerfully laid aside his gold-laced hat, lest, as he said, it should make him too proud; and stripped himself of his bright-hued waistcoat, for with that on his back, he told Bennet Langton, he "could not treat people with the same ease as when in his usual plain clothes." He had the satisfaction of seeing his tragedy published, and had the pleasure of receiving one hundred pounds for the copyright. His friendship for Garrick abided to the end, and for a considerable time he continued to frequent the greenroom of Drury Lane, until he began to fear the gay company he invariably found there should lead him into temptation. Then he said to Garrick, "I'll come no more behind your scenes, David; for the silk stockings and white bosoms of your actresses excite my amorous propensities."

# OLIVER GOLDSMITH'S SHE STOOPS TO CONQUER.

### FIRST PRODUCED, 15TH MARCH, 1773.

Goldsmith Consults a Friend—A Varied Life—Brighter Days—In Tom Davies' Shop—A Dramatist's Difficulties—*The Good-natured Man*—Oliver Goldsmith and David Garrick—Misunderstandings—A Rejected Manuscript—Letters to Colman and Garrick—Writing a New Comedy—Appealing to Managers—Hard Treatment—Johnson's Friendship—Goldsmith's Despondency—First Night of *She Stoops to Conquer*—Success and Criticism.

# OLIVER GOLDSMITH'S SHE STOOPS TO CONQUER.

WILLIAM COOKE, Esquire, barrister-at-law, and author of a didactic poem, relates that his friend and neighbour, Oliver Goldsmith, met an old acquaintance at a chop-house soon after he had finished his comedy, then unnamed, but subsequently known as *She Stoops to Conquer; or, The Mistakes of a Night*. And with him the ingenious writer fell into confidential discourse concerning his play, of which he begged his honest opinion as a friend on whose word he relied, as a critic in whose judgment he trusted. Therefore, in his "strange, uncouth, deranged manner," Goldsmith laid bare the plot, which his hearer understood turned upon one gentleman mistaking the house of another for an inn. This device, his critic believed, was one the public, "under their then sentimental impressions," would think too broad and farcical for comedy. Hearing which, Goldsmith, who, like all poets, was alternately sanguine and despondent, looked most serious. Then, seizing his friend's hand, he "piteously exclaimed," he was much obliged for his candid opinion; "but," he continued, "it is all I can do; for, alas, I find that my genius, if ever I had any, has of late totally deserted me!"

This happened in the spring of 1772, when Goldsmith's age numbered forty-four years, most of which had been spent in toil and trouble. Sixteen years previously he had returned from those strange, eventful travels abroad, where he had experienced such humiliations as were produced by "living on the hospitalities of the friars in convents, sleeping in barns, and picking up a kind of mendicant livelihood by the German flute with great pleasantry." Meanwhile he had played many parts upon life's stage. During the night of misery preceding the dawn of his prosperity, he had herded with the beggars of Axe Lane;

mixed medicines, spread ointments, and run of errands for Jacob, a poor apothecary in Monument Yard ; became a physician " in a humble way ; " corrected proofs for the press of Samuel Richardson, printer and author ; taught in a polite academy for young gentlemen at Peckham ; contributed to Griffith's *Monthly Review;* returned starving and miserable to resume his ushership ; and began his career as an author by writing a series of papers for the columns of the *Public Ledger,* called *Chinese Letters,* reprinted under the title of *The Citizen of the World.*

Then came brighter days. From reviewing books he fell to writing them ; from occupying a garret in Green Arbour Court near the Old Bailey, he rose to chambers in the Temple. Moreover, the companionship of beggars in Axe Lane was exchanged for association with men of learning and parts, who, loving the simplicity of his nature, valued the worth of his genius. Accordingly, he became a frequent visitor to the shop of Tom Davies, an unsuccessful player, who, renouncing the stage, became a prosperous bookseller and publisher. His shop, located in Russell Street, Covent Garden, was famous as a resort for actors and authors, poets and patrons, wits and gossips. Here Boswell met Johnson; young Mr. Reynolds, the painter, discoursed with the admired author of Night Thoughts; Foote mimicked Garrick; and George Colman, Richard Cumberland, Hugh Kelly, and Arthur Murphy, playwrights all, debated on the condition and prospects of the drama with George Steevens, Esq., a cynic by nature, a critic by profession.*

Here the fortunes of a play were frequently decided, the value of a book declared, the fate of an author determined. The potent-voiced central figure of the brilliant group congregating on these premises, was the ex-player, who, as Steevens wrote Garrick, was "to the full as much

---

* Here, likewise, was it, Johnson, hearing of Foote's intention to caricature him on the stage, asked Davies: " What is the price of a common ash stick, sir ? " " Sixpence," answered the bookseller. " Why, then, sir," exclaimed the philosopher, " give me leave to send your servant to purchase me a shilling one. I'll have a double quantity; for I am told Foote means to take me off, as he calls it, and I am determined the fellow shall not do it with impunity."

a king in his own shop as ever he was on your stage. When·he was on the point of leaving the theatre," continues the critic, "he most certainly stole some copper diadem from a shelf, and put it in his pocket. He has worn it ever since." Recognising Goldsmith's genius, he had bidden him attend his levees, and the poet was proud to associate with the frequenters of the bookseller's shop.

It was not conversation concerning literature, exchanged by Davies' friends, which alone possessed keen interest for Goldsmith's mind; all topics regarding the theatre exercised a fascination for him, little suspected by his acquaintances. The stage had, indeed, ever proved a source of great attraction and innocent delight to him in the past; it was destined to become a centre of brief triumph and a source of bitter humiliation to him in the future. A proof his talents had early inclined towards the drama remains in the fact of his having written part of a tragedy in his days of struggle and privation. And now, having achieved success as author of The Vicar of Wakefield and The Traveller, and possessing

L

a reputation for elegance, humour, and pathos, he resolved on writing a comedy. This determination was quickened to fulfilment by the success of *The Clandestine Marriage*, a joint composition of David Garrick and George Colman.

Nor was Goldsmith unaware of the difficulties besetting a dramatist's path. In the previous decade, a reaction from the gross indecencies of Dryden, Wycherley, and Congreve had set in; and a species of play, introduced by Steele, known as sentimental comedy, held possession of the stage. From this school of dramatic writing Goldsmith was resolved to depart, and determined to portray life in a manner true to nature.

But before he could succeed in presenting his play to the town for approval, it was necessary he should first gain favour with the managers of Drury Lane or Covent Garden theatres. Of the obstacles here awaiting him he was well convinced. Indeed, in his Enquiry into Polite Literature, he had already devoted a chapter to the subject.

"A drama," he said, "must undergo a pro-

cess truly chemical before it is presented to
the public. It must be tried in the manager's
fire, strained through a licenser, suffer from repeated corrections till it may be a mere *caput
mortuum* when it arrives before the public. . . .
Old pieces are revived and scarce any new ones
admitted. The actor is ever in our eye, the
poet seldom permitted to appear, and the
stage, instead of serving the people, is made
subservient to the interests of avarice. Getting
a play on, even in three or four years, is a
privilege reserved only for the happy few who
have the arts of courting the manager as well
as the Muse; who have adulation to please his
vanity, powerful patrons to support their merit,
or money to indemnify disappointment. Our
Saxon ancestors had but one name for a wit
and a witch. I will not dispute the propriety
of uniting those characters then; but the man
who, under the present discouragements, ventures
to write for the stage, whatever claim he may
have to the appellation of a wit, at least has
no right to be called a conjuror."

L 2

However, Goldsmith determined to try his fortune as a dramatist, and whilst his first comedy, *The Good-natured Man*, was in progress, decided on offering it to Rich, then lessee of Covent Garden Theatre. The manager's death occurring at this period, and his affairs being thrown into confusion, Goldsmith next resolved on submitting his play to Garrick's consideration. Unfortunately a misunderstanding had arisen between poet and player, which suspended kindly feeling on either side. Shortly after the publication of Goldsmith's remarks concerning the stage, he had striven to obtain a vacant secretaryship of the Society of Arts, and had personally canvassed the great Mr. Garrick for his vote. On this occasion the actor, with some show of indignation, replied it was impossible Dr. Goldsmith could lay claim to any recommendation from him, having taken pains to deprive himself of his assistance, by an unprovoked attack upon his management of the theatre. The poor author, not dreaming of making an apology, replied simply enough that "in truth had spoken his mind, and believed what he said was very right."

Hearing this, Garrick dismissed him with civility, and Goldsmith lost the office he sought.

After this interview the poet and the player avoided each other's company; and though possessing many mutual friends, did not meet until kindly Joshua Reynolds brought them together in the drawing-room of his house in Leicester Square, that Goldsmith might place his manuscript of *The Good-natured Man* in Garrick's hands. Their meeting lacked the cordiality which foreruns friendship. Davies, in his Life of Garrick, speaking of this occasion, says the manager "was fully conscious of his merit, and perhaps more ostentatious of his abilities to serve a dramatic author than became a man of prudence," whilst Goldsmith, on the other hand, was no less persuaded of his own importance, and anxious to assert his independence. " Mr. Garrick, "writes Tom Davies, "who had been so long treated with the complimentary language paid to a successful patentee and admired actor,. expected that the writer would esteem the patronage of his play a favour; Goldsmith rejected all ideas of kindness in a bargain that was in-

tended to be of mutual advantage to both, and
in this was certainly justifiable. I believe the
manager was willing to accept the play, but he
wished to be courted to it ; and the Doctor was
not disposed to purchase his friendship by the
resignation of his sincerity." The original breach
therefore remained unbridged ; and when presently David Garrick took his leave with many
smiles, the distressed poet muttered "he could
not suffer such airs of superiority from one who
was only a poor player." To which Joshua
Reynolds replied : " No, no, don't say that; he
is no poor player surely."

The manuscript of *The Good-natured Man* remained in Garrick's keeping a considerable time,
during which Goldsmith chafed at the strain to
which his patience was subjected. At first the
manager regarded the comedy with favourable
eyes, whilst he took care, as Sir James Prior
states, "not to express himself so frankly, as to
be unable to retreat from any rash inferences of
the author." Hesitation and prevarication followed. Goldsmith was led to anticipate success
for his work, whilst Joshua Reynolds and John-

son were assured it would never gain public esteem. Meanwhile Goldsmith battled with book-sellers, and slaved for editors that he might earn daily bread; and at last, harassed by un-merciful circumstances, he took heart to ask, in hopes of future success, that the great manager would lend him a little money upon his note, a request immediately granted. Interviews at Garrick's house were now held, when he sug-gested certain alterations and amendments to which the author strongly objected. And no prospect of mutual understanding being visible, Garrick proposed the comedy should be sub-mitted to the opinion of his reader, White-head, the Poet Laureate, or others. This in-censed Goldsmith thoroughly, who concluded the manager had canvassed his friends for their unfavourable opinions of the comedy. He therefore vented his feelings in expressions of anger, whilst Garrick, serene and affable, loftily assured him " he felt more pains in giving words to his sentiments than Dr. Goldsmith could possibly have in receiving them."

The last days of June, 1767, were now at

hand, and Garrick left London to visit his native town, Lichfield. The fate of Goldsmith's play was yet undetermined, but an event had recently happened which caused him to look hopefully towards its acceptance by another house. Some months after the demise of Rich, George Colman purchased a fourth share in Covent Garden Theatre, and became its manager. To him ·Goldsmith forwarded his comedy, and in return speedily received some sorely needed words of encouragement. The poor playwright's spirit revived, his gratitude overflowed. "I am very much obliged to you," he writes to Colman on the 19th July, "both for your kind partiality in my favour and your tenderness in shortening the interval of my expectation. That the play is liable to many objections I well know, but I am happy that it is in hands the most capable in the world of removing them. If then, dear sir, you will complete your favours by putting the piece into such a state as it may be acted, or of directing me how to do it, I shall ever retain a sense of your goodness to me. And, indeed, though most probable this be the last I shall ever write, yet

I can't help feeling a secret satisfaction that poets for the future are likely to have a protector who declines taking advantage of their dependent situation, and scorns that importance which may be acquired by trifling with their anxieties."

Having placed his comedy in the hands of a rival manager, he wrote to inform Garrick of his action. He had forwarded the play to Covent Garden, he said, "thinking it wrong to take up the attention of my friends with such petty concerns as mine, or to load your good nature by a compliance rather with their requests than my merits. I am extremely sorry," he continues, "that you should think me warm at our last meeting; your judgment certainly ought to be free, especially in a matter which must in some measure concern your own credit and interest." He then states he had no disposition to differ with him on this or any other account, and he entertained a high opinion of his abilities and a real esteem for his person. Garrick's reply was generous and courteous: "I was indeed much hurt," he says, "that your warmth at our last meeting mistook my sincere and friendly attention to your play, for the remains of a former misunderstanding which I had as much forgot as if it had never existed. . . . It has been the business, and ever will be, of my life, to live on the best terms with men of genius; and I know that Dr. Goldsmith will have no reason to change his previous friendly disposition towards me, as I shall be glad of every future opportunity to convince him how much I am his obedient servant and well-wisher."

In due time *The Good-natured Man* was accepted, but five slow months passed before it was produced. For this delay there were several excuses. Disputes arose between the proprietors of the theatre; disagreement followed concerning the lady selected to represent the heroine; some of the actors protested against the characters for which they were cast; and finally Colman abandoned all hope of success for the play. Ultimately it was produced on the 29th of January, 1768. On the first representation its popularity was not assured, but it ran for ten nights, and was much commended for striking originality and hearty humour.

Inasmuch as the incidents just narrated regarding *The Good-natured Man* bear on the production of Goldsmith's second and more important comedy, place is given them in these pages. Though he had intimated his first play should be his last, he was again tempted to write for the stage by knowledge of the honours and profits awaiting successful dramatists. But whilst strongly desirous of popularity in this line of art, and of the resulting gains he sadly needed, he was resolved to again combat the public taste for sentimental comedy, and hunt, as he expressed himself, "after nature and humour in whatever walks of life they were most conspicuous." That he might be freer from interruptions whilst engaged in writing the comedy, he took lodgings in a farmhouse, situated in Hyde Lane, close to the pretty village of Hyde, and six miles removed from London. For him the country possessed inexhaustible charms; the voice of nature found reverent echo in his heart; the peace of pastoral life soothed, refreshed, and inspired him. He had more than once, when oppressed by work and bewildered with care, fled from Fleet Street, with its dark bookshops, noisy taverns, and crowded ordinaries, to take refuge in Islington, which then boasted its green fields and pleasant lanes.   He had likewise, in company with his friend Bott, taken a house on the Edgware Road, some eight miles removed from town, where he wrote his History of Rome. And when, through stress of circumstances, he could not afford the luxury of a country lodging, he stole some hours from work that he might spend them in the purer atmosphere of the suburbs.   This relaxation he called his shoe-maker's holiday.   William Cooke quaintly describes the innocent manner in which these holidays were passed.   At ten o'clock in the morning three or four of the author's intimate friends met at his chambers; at eleven they proceeded by the City Road and through green fields to Highbury Barn.   Here an excellent ordinary, consisting of two dishes and pastry, was served, at tenpence a-head, including a penny to the waiter; the company generally consisting of a few Templars, some literary men, and citizens retired from trade. About six o'clock in the evening Goldsmith and his friends adjourned to White Conduit House, where they drank tea ; and concluded a pleasant excursion by supping at the Grecian or Temple Exchange Coffee Houses, or at the Globe in Fleet Street. The whole expenses of the day never exceeded a crown, but generally amounted to three shillings and sixpence or four shillings each.

Having in contemplation the comedy destined to delight, not merely his own, but succeeding generations, he once more sought retirement in the country, and hired a room in Hyde Lane farmhouse.* After months of toil and anxiety

---

* Some months ago I went in search of the homestead where the poet lodged ; and arriving at Hyde Lane, a charming locality gradually rising on a hillside, bordered by thick hedges and commanding a prospect of peaceful meadow-lands, I hesitated as to which of two houses standing not far apart, was sacred to the poet's shade. The place seemed deserted ; no sound of life disturbed the noonday quiet, until the figure of a postman with an empty bag upon his back, whistling as he walked for want of letters, came in sight. To him I addressed myself inquiringly, begging he would inform me in which of these houses Goldsmith had lived. A thoughtful expression crossed his

he rested here as in a haven of contentment. His days were chiefly spent in his room, where his meals were served, that continuous work might be uninterrupted. At times—his stooping figure attired in an old dressing-gown, his neck exposed by a wide open collar, his feet encased in worn slippers — he sauntered into the kitchen, and taking his position on the wide, open hearth, pleasantly conversed with the household, or remained silent and abstracted, till some thought flashing through his mind, he hurried away to record it instantly. Occasionally, when days were fair, he wandered about the neighbouring fields, sometimes with a volume in his hand, and again loitered in the shade of hedgerows, lost in thought. At intervals he journeyed to town, tarrying there for days, and now and then Dr. Johnson, Joshua Reynolds, and Sir William Chambers visited him,

---

vacant face. "Mr. Goldsmith?" said he. "Well, I don't remember the name of such a gentleman, and I've been in this district three years. He must have lived here before my time." I gravely replied he had, and we parted with many expressions of mutual civility. I succeeded in identifying the house, and in seeing the apartment in the upper storey, where *She Stoops to Conquer* was written.

when they drank tea, and told excellent stories, in the prim parlour placed at their service for such entertainments.

Meanwhile his comedy drew towards its close, and early in the year 1772 Goldsmith was back in London, battling with booksellers, labouring to surmount financial difficulties, and striving to get his play accepted. He had submitted it to George Colman ; but tedious weeks and lingering months wore away, and no satisfactory answer was returned to the expectant author. Spring passed and brought him no hope ; summer came, and he lay prostrate from illness. With the reopening of the theatrical season in autumn his expectations rose again, only to meet with disappointment once more. At last, harassed by doubts and beset by difficulties, he wrote the following pathetic letter to George Colman, in January, 1773 :

"DEAR SIR,

"I entreat you will deliver me from that state of suspense in which I have been kept for a long time. Whatever objections you have made or shall make to my play, I will endeavour to

remove and not argue about them. To bring in
any new judges either of its merits or faults I can
never submit to. Upon a former occasion when
my other play was before Mr. Garrick, he offered
to bring me before Mr. Whitehead's tribunal, but I
refused the proposal with indignation. I hope I
shall not experience as hard treatment from you
as from him. I have, as you know, a large sum
of money to make up shortly; by accepting my
play I can readily satisfy my creditor that way; at
any rate I must look about to some certainty to be
prepared. For God's sake take the play and let
us make the best of it, and let me have the same
measure at least which you have given as bad
plays as mine.

" I am, your friend and servant,

"OLIVER GOLDSMITH."


In answer to this appeal his manuscript was
returned, with various remarks and proposed
alterations scribbled over the blank sides of its
pages; it was accompanied by a note, stating
that notwithstanding its blemishes the play would
be produced. Feeling the hardship of this treat-

ment he was powerless to resent, Goldsmith sent his comedy, with the corrections thick upon its pages, to Garrick. Constant intercourse between actor and author at Joshua Reynolds' house had made them better acquainted, and helped to establish kindly feelings in which past hostility was happily forgotten in present friendship.. Therefore the poet had hopes his play would be produced at Drury Lane ; but before Garrick had time to arrive at conclusions concerning it, Goldsmith, acting on Johnson's advice, requested the manuscript might be returned.

"I ask many pardons for the trouble I gave you yesterday," he wrote. " Upon more mature deliberation, and the advice of a sensible friend, I began to think it indelicate in me to throw upon you the odium of confirming Mr. Colman's sentence. I therefore request you will send my play back by my servant, for having been assured of having it acted at the other house, though I confess yours in every respect more to my wish, yet it would be folly in me to forego an advantage which lies in my power of appealing from Mr. Colman's opinion to the judgment of the town.

M

I entreat, if not too late, you will keep this affair
a secret for some time."

Garrick having returned the manuscript,
Johnson, ever anxious to serve his friend, waited
on Colman, "who was prevailed on at last by
much solicitation, nay, by a kind of force, to bring
it on." The time fixed for its production was
March.

Colman, accepting the comedy against his will,
predicted its ill-success, and his tone was speedily
adopted by some members of his company. Mrs.
Abington, Gentleman Smith, and Woodward—
three of the principal players, for whom the characters of Miss Hardcastle, Marlow, and Tony
Lumpkin were respectively intended—declined
their parts. This was a severe blow to Goldsmith,
who had boasted of creating the heroine to suit
Mrs. Abington's personality and, moreover,
expected much help from Smith and Woodward's talent. The motive instigating their
conduct may be judged from a subsequent con-
fession of the latter, who declared he was influ-
enced by the manager's opinion that the comedy
would never reach a second performance. In this

dilemma Shuter, who had rendered Goldsmith much service in *The Good-natured Man*, proposed an actor named Lewes should represent Young Marlow; but to this the author was unwilling to consent, Lewes being principally employed as a harlequin, and but seldom entrusted with speaking parts. Shuter was, however, of opinion Lewes had talents which merely required opportunity for development. Therefore he had frequently urged him to throw down the mask and don the buskin. He now assured him there was a part in the new comedy befitting his abilities, which Smith had declined, and at the same time besought Goldsmith to entrust Lewes with the character of Young Marlow. To this the playwright consented with some reluctance, but seeing him at rehearsal declared that next to Shuter, who played Hardcastle, Lewes's was the best performance. Miss Hardcastle was allotted to Mrs. Bulkley, and Tony Lumpkin to Quick. The cast, with the exceptions mentioned, proving most indifferent, Goldsmith's friends urged him to postpone the performance of his comedy until autumn, when probably the better members of the company might reconsider their judgment. But he answered stoutly, "I should rather that my play were damned by bad players, than merely saved by good acting."

Therefore the rehearsals were continued in a dispirited manner, when Colman occasionally suggested fresh alterations, now accepted, and again rejected by the suffering author. Nor was the manager willing to avert the apprehended failure by incurring the slightest expense for scenery or clothes. Stock scenes which had seen active service, and old dresses taken from the general wardrobe, were reintroduced. Occasionally these gloomy rehearsals were brightened by the presence of the playwright's friends. Here in front of the semi-lit stage sat ponderous Johnson, surrounded by Joshua Reynolds and his sister, the Horneck family, Edmund Burke, and Arthur Murphy, all being ready to offer suggestions and express comments.

And now, though the night of its first appearance was fast approaching, no name had been given the comedy. Various titles were proposed. "We are all in labour," writes Johnson, "for a name for Goldy's play." Joshua Reynolds suggested *The Belle's Stratagem*—afterwards used by Mrs. Cowley for one of her comedies—and playfully assured Goldsmith if it were not used, he would exert his utmost endeavours to damn the production. Another friend considered *The Old House a New Inn,* more suitable; but the author finally selected *She Stoops to Conquer; or, The Mistakes of a Night,* as the most appropriate title. Nor did difficulties connected with the representation of this comedy now end; but on the contrary, seemingly concentrated themselves in a final effort to bewilder and overwhelm poor Goldsmith. Garrick, by way of proving his friendship towards the author, wrote an excellent prologue for the new play, and Arthur Murphy supplied an epilogue. The latter, it was intended, should be sung by Miss Catley. Becoming aware of this, Mrs. Bulkley protested, if she were not allowed to speak the lines, she would not play the heroine. By way of pacifying them Goldsmith wrote a "quarrelling epilogue;" in this both were intended to take part, and debate as to which should speak the piece. This compromise Miss Catley in her turn flatly refused. The distracted poet then penned an epilogue for Mrs. Bulkley, to which Colman objected, inasmuch as he considered it lacked merit, when Goldsmith finally wrote another, that was ultimately accepted. "Such," he writes to his friend Cradock, "is the history of my stage adventures, and which I have at last done with. I cannot help saying that I am very sick of the stage, and though I believe I shall get three tolerable benefits, yet I shall on the whole be a loser, even in a pecuniary light; my ease and comfort I certainly lost while it was in agitation."

As the date fixed for the production of his play drew near, gloomiest anticipations of its fate were entertained. Its plot was considered decidedly low; its humour was thought extremely vulgar; and, from the first scene to the last, it betrayed an absence of those moral maxims and vapid sentiments dear to public taste. However, some hope lay in the fact that an innovation occurred in theatrical representations about this time, which helped to prepare the town for his comedy. On the 15th of February, Samuel Foote,

the incarnate genius of satire, had opened his
theatre in the Haymarket for the spring season,
with an entertainment he was pleased to call a
"Primitive Puppet Show," which ridiculed sentimental comedy in the most glaring manner. The
production by which Foote's company of so-called
puppets sought to accomplish this end was entitled
*The Handsome Housemaid; or, Piety in Pattens.*
The audiences witnessing this merry comedy
"tasted," says the *General Evening Post,* "the
salt of satire ; they saw the evident intention of
the burlesque upon modern comedy ; they confessed that a dull truth, stripped of its artificial
guise of words, was the offence of the generality
of those sentiments the writers of the present
age lard their pieces with; and, convinced of
having adopted a false taste, they joined in their
own verdict by loudly approving what may justly
be termed Foote's mirror for sentimental writers."
The town, having seen this performance and
laughed at its vagaries, was better prepared to
appreciate a comedy which copied nature.

At last the 15th March, 1773, the date fixed
for the first representation of *She Stoops to*

*Conquer,* arrived. Goldsmith's friends, resolving to celebrate the day as became its importance, agreed to dine in company before visiting the playhouse. George Steevens, who was to form one of that goodly group, whilst on his way to dinner* called for Dr. Johnson, whom he found attired in bright colours. The court was then in mourning for the King of Sardinia, and, it being customary for all loyal subjects to wear sober black in public places during such periods, Steevens reminded him of the fact. On this, the burly philosopher hastened to change his suit, the while giving vent to his gratitude for "information that had saved him from an appearance so improper in the front row of a front box." He would not, he declared, "for ten pounds have seemed so retrograde to any general observance." Being clad in neutral hues, he accompanied Steevens to the dinner, where they met Joshua Reynolds, Edmund and Richard

---

* Cumberland, who is usually incorrect, states this was held at the "Shakespeare Tavern;" Northcote, Sir Joshua's pupil, told Sir James Prior it took place at the great painter's house.

Burke, Caleb Whitefoord, Major Mills, and Gold-smith.

And now the hour of trial, long anticipated and greatly feared, being at hand, the poor play-wright was nervous beyond expression. His fame as a writer could scarce be injured by his failure as a dramatist; but he was strongly desirous of success, the more as his straitened finances caused him bitter distress. Accordingly, at dinner, he was by turns extravagantly mirthful and pro-foundly depressed. The friendly sallies of Johnson, the hopeful prognostications of courteous Sir Joshua, the epigrammatic speeches of Edmund Burke, were unable to divert his thoughts or calm his feverish excitement; and his mouth, as Northcote states, "became so parched and dry from the agitation of his mind, that he was unable to swallow a single mouthful."

When dinner was over, and glasses were drained to his prosperity, the party started for Covent Garden; but Goldsmith declined accompanying his friends, for, unable to bear the strain of wit-nessing the performance, he resolved on absenting himself from the theatre until the fate of his comedy was assured. Meanwhile the playhouse, having opened its doors at five o'clock, was speedily filled by an eager and expectant crowd. The various perplexing delays in the production of the comedy had been freely canvassed in Tom Davies' shop, and in ordinaries and taverns throughout the town. As a result, the manager's behaviour was set down to the jealousy of a rival playwright, and strong sympathy had arisen in favour of the distressed author. This feeling found practical expression in a thronged house. At six o'clock the curtain rose, when Woodward appeared dressed in mourning, with a white handkerchief applied to his eyes, weeping for the fate of Miss Comedy, who, he explained in the words of the prologue, was just expiring. Therefore did he entertain sore fears for himself and his brother comedians ; however, he had some hopes of her ultimate recovery, as a certain well-known doctor had come to her relief, and it rested with the audience to pronounce whether he was a quack or a regular practitioner.

Then the play began, and an eager house, catching the humour of its scenes and appreciating the wit of its dialogue, quickly warmed into hearty merriment. By degrees, the actors' fears subsided, and, the feelings of their audience being magnetically communicated to them, their parts became invested with new interest. Northcote, who was in the gallery with Sir Joshua's "confidential man," says after the second act, no doubt existed of the comedy's success. All eyes were turned upon Johnson, sitting in the front row of a box, "and when he laughed everybody thought himself entitled to roar." Enjoyment and good humour were contagious. Tony Lumpkin's antics and Marlow's mistakes set the house in excellent humour. The while Goldsmith, hoping little and fearing much, wandered moodily in St. James's Park, where he was met by a friend, who, remonstrating with him on his absence from the playhouse, and representing " how useful his presence might be in making some sudden alterations which might be found necessary in the piece," prevailed on him to visit the theatre. Accordingly he bent his steps towards Covent Garden, and timorously crossed the threshold of the stage door. As he reached the wings, a solitary hiss fell upon his ear.

This was evoked by the supposed improbability of Mrs. Hardcastle believing herself forty miles distant from her home, though standing in her own gardens, a deception actually practised by Sheridan on Madame de Genlis. Hearing this ominous sound Goldsmith started in terror. "What's that?" he said to Colman, who stood beside him. " Psha," replied the manager, wrathful that his prophecies of failure had been falsified, " don't be fearful of squibs when we have been sitting these two hours on a barrel of gunpowder." * The heartless cruelty and injustice of this speech were never forgotten by the author, who, hearing the immoderate laughter and loud applause which quickly followed, was speedily assured of his success.

This happy result was in some measure due to the excellent acting of Shuter and Lewes, whose merits are extolled in the columns of the *Morning Chronicle* and *London Advertiser* of the following day.

---

* A different version of this story states that Colman's remark was made at one of the rehearsals ; but Cooke, who heard it from Goldsmith, avers it occurred as stated above.

Between the night of its first performance and the close of the season, in consequence of holidays, and benefits, when actors selected their own pieces, but twelve nights remained at the manager's disposal. On these, *She Stoops to Conquer* was played to crowded houses and with increasing popularity. "The applause given to a new piece on the first evening of its representation," says the *Public Advertiser*, "is sometimes supposed to be the tribute of partial friendship, but the approbation shown on the second exhibition of Dr. Goldsmith's new comedy exceeded that with which its first appearance was attended. Uninterrupted laughter and clamorous plaudits accompanied his muse to the last line of the play; and when it was given out for the author's benefit, the theatre was filled with the loudest acclamations that ever rung within its walls."

Its success was moreover doubly assured from being witnessed on the tenth night of its production by George III.; and receiving a most favourable verdict from Johnson. "I know of no comedy for many years," said he, "that has so much exhilarated an audience — that has answered so much the great end of comedy— making an audience merry." That His Majesty would honour the play with his presence was a compliment Goldsmith strongly desired. "I wish he would, not that it would do me the least good," he said, "with affected indifference," according to Boswell. "Well then, sir," replied Johnson, laughing, "let us say it would do him good. No, sir, this affectation will not pass, it is mighty idle. In such a state as ours, who would not wish to please the chief magistrate?"

The three benefit nights allowed Goldsmith brought him the welcome sum of between three and four hundred pounds. The copyright of his comedy was then given to Francis Newbery, of St. Paul's Churchyard, by way of paying certain moneys amounting to between two and three hundred pounds, which had been advanced by him to Goldsmith. Its sale surprised both author and publisher, six thousand copies being disposed of in a few months, by which Newbery profited over three hundred pounds. The comedy was dedicated to Johnson in terms of affection

and respect. "In inscribing this slight performance to you," he wrote, "I do not mean so
much to compliment you as myself. It may do
me some honour to inform the public that I
have lived many years in intimacy with you.
It may serve the interests of mankind also to
inform them that the greatest wit may be found
in a character without impairing the most un-
affected piety."

Amongst the general applause which greeted
the comedy, two dissenting voices were heard.
These proceeded from Ralph Griffiths, editor of
the *Monthly Review*, and Horace Walpole, the
superfine critic, of Strawberry Hill. The former
declared "the merit of *She Stoops to Conquer* consisted in that sort of dialogue which lies on a
level with the most common understandings, and
in that low mischief and mirth which we laugh
at while we are ready to despise ourselves for
so doing." Horace Walpole, who, because his
father had been attacked by Goldsmith, detested
the author, is yet more severe regarding the
play. "Dr. Goldsmith has written a comedy,"
he tells the Rev. William Mason: "no, it is the

lowest of all farces. It is not the subject I condemn, though very vulgar, but the execution.
The drift tends to no moral, to no edification
of any kind. The situations, however, are well
imagined, and make one laugh, in spite of the
grossness of the dialogue, the forced witticisms,
and total improbability of the whole plan and
conduct. But what disgusts me most is that,
though the characters are very low, and aim at
low humour, not one of them says a sentence
that is natural or marks any character at all.
It is set up in opposition to sentimental comedy,
and is as bad as the worst of them." Such a
criticism, whilst shaming its writer's memory, is
powerless to injure the playwright's fame.

It seemed as if sentimental comedy had now
received its death-blow. The journals teemed
with squibs intended to burlesque the old school
and commend the new, one characteristic speci-
men of which will be sufficient to indicate their
general tone. Under the heading of Theatrical
Intelligence, the *Morning Chronicle*, on the occasion of Goldsmith's third benefit night, gravely
states: "It is with much pleasure we can inform

the public that the ingenious and engaging Miss Comedy is in a fair way of recovery. This much admired young lady has lately been in a very declining way, and was thought to be dying of a sentimental consumption. She is now under the care of Dr. Goldsmith, who has already pre-scribed twice for her. The medicines sat extremely easy upon her stomach, and she appears to be in fine spirits. The Doctor is to pay her a third visit this evening, and it is expected he will receive a very handsome fee from the lady's friends and admirers."

In the midst of Goldsmith's success the humi-liation and pain Colman had inflicted were not forgotten. Letters, lampoons, and paragraphs, censuring and condemning the unhappy manager, appeared in the public prints. In making such attacks the writers not only joined in universal condemnation of Colman, but probably avenged mortifications they had likewise suffered at his hands. His criticisms on *She Stoops to Conquer* were repeated to incite ridicule and produce laughter; his suggestions were attributed to jealousy; his judgment was regarded with contempt. How could future playwrights, it was asked, offer pieces to a manager so deficient in discrimination, so wanting in appreciation ? The town jeered at him, and its merriment was continually fed with fresh satires. The *Morning Chronicle* of March 24th says : "The multitude of epigrams, verses, paragraphs, letters, etc., which we have received on the subject of Dr. Goldsmith's new play, the manager's behaviour, etc., shall be inserted in their turn as fast as possible." They fell upon Colman with dire effect.

"The comedy of *She Stoops to Conquer*," says one writer, addressing him, "has triumphed over all your paltry efforts to bespeak its condemnation ; efforts in which the envy of the author was no less conspicuous than the duplicity of the manager. . . . Mr. Foote has hung you out to ridicule at the conclusion of his Puppet Show. Every newspaper encourages the laugh against you—so that Colman's judgment will become a proverbial expression to signify no judgment at all. Every friend of Dr. Goldsmith's insists on his having no further connection with you, and Mr. Lewes is much too negligent of his own interests, if he does not speedily demand to have his salary raised on account of the consequence he has derived from a piece, which you were willing to persuade the world would never appear a second time on the stage."

At last, bewildered and overcome by repeated attacks,* Colman left town and sought peace at Bath, from where, "being so distressed with abuse," he solicited Goldsmith, as Johnson writes, "to take him off the rack of the newspapers." With this

---

* One of the most humorous satires ran as follows :

Come, Coley, doff those mourning weeds,
  Nor thus with jokes be flamm'd ;
Tho' Goldsmith's present play succeeds,
  His next may still be damn'd.
As this has 'scap'd without a fall,
  To sink his next prepare ;
New actors hire from Wapping Wall
  And dresses from Rag Fair.

For scenes let tatter'd blankets fly,
  The prologue Kelly write,
Then swear again the piece must die
  Before the author's night.
Should these tricks fail the lucky elf
  To bring to lasting shame,
E'en write the best you can yourself,
  And print it in his name.

wish the forgiving playwright, who had taken
no part in the assaults, was quite willing to comply. "The undertaking of a comedy not merely
sentimental, was very dangerous," he said to his
friends, "and Mr. Colman, who saw this piece in
its various stages, always thought it so. However,
I ventured to trust it to the public; and though
it was necessarily delayed until late in the season,
I have every reason to be grateful."

Goldsmith's triumph was, however, attended
by envy; his joy was mixed with pain, the chief
cause being a gross attack made upon him
in the *London Packet*. To accurately judge of
its scurrility and offensiveness it must be read
verbatim: "Sir," it began, "the happy knack
which you have learnt of puffing your own com-
positions provokes me to come forth. You have
not been the editor of newspapers and magazines
not to discover the trick of literary humbug. But
the gauze is so thin that the very foolish part
of the world see through it and discover the
doctor's monkey face and cloven foot. Your
poetic vanity is as unpardonable as your personal.
Would man believe it, and will woman bear it,

to be told that for hours the great Goldsmith will stand surveying his grotesque ourang-outang figure in a pier-glass? Was not the lovely Horneck as much enamoured, you would not sigh, my gentle swain, in vain. But your vanity is preposterous. How will the same bard of Bedlam ring the changes in praise of Goldy? But what has he to be either proud or vain of? The Traveller is a flimsy poem, built upon false principles, principles diametrically opposite to liberty. What is *The Good-natured Man* but a poor water-gruel dramatic dose? What is The Deserted Village but a pretty poem of easy numbers, without fancy, dignity, genius, or fire? And pray what may be the last speaking pantomime, so praised by the doctor himself, but an incoherent piece of stuff, the figure of a woman with a fish's tail, without plot, incident, or intrigue? We are made to laugh at stale, dull jokes, wherein we mistake pleasantry for wit, and grimace for humour; wherein every scene is unnatural and inconsistent with the rules, the laws of nature and of the drama, viz., the gentlemen come to a man of fortune's house, eat, drink, sleep, and take it for an inn.

The one is intended as a lover to the daughter; he talks with her for some hours, and when he sees her again in a different dress he treats her as a bar-girl, and swears she squinted. He abuses the master of the house, and threatens to kick him out of his own doors. The squire, whom we are told is to be a fool, proves the most sensible being of the piece; and he makes out a whole act by bidding his mother lie close behind a bush, persuading her that his father—her own husband —is a highwayman, and that he is come to cut their throats; and, to give his cousin an opportunity to go off, he drives his mother over hedges, ditches, and through ponds. There is not, sweet, sucking Johnson, a natural stroke in the whole play but the young fellow's giving the stolen jewels to the mother, supposing her to be the landlady. That Mr. Colman did no justice to this piece I honestly allow; that he told all his friends it would be damned I positively aver; and from such ungenerous insinuations, without a dramatic merit, it rose to public notice, and it is now the *ton* to go see it, though I never saw a person that either liked or approved it. Mr.

Goldsmith, correct your arrogance, reduce your vanity, and endeavour to believe as a man you are of the plainest sort, 'and as an author but a mortal piece of mediocrity.

> Brise le miroir infidèle
> Qui vous cache la vérité.

> " TOM TICKLE."

This letter escaped Goldsmith's notice until his friend Captain Higgins, an Irishman possessing the national love of warfare, acquainted him of its existence, and contended it was but just the writer should receive corporal punishment. There was not much difficulty in persuading the abused author to agree with him in this conviction, and therefore, accompanied by the gallant captain, he directed his steps towards Paternoster Row, where the *London Packet* was published by Evans. Entering the shop, he demanded to see the latter, who immediately came forward from an adjoining room. Addressing him, the poet said his name was Goldsmith, and he had called in consequence of a scurrilous attack upon him, and an unwarrantable liberty taken with the name of a young lady

in the *London Packet.* "As for myself, I care
little," he exclaimed, "but her name must not
be sported with." Declaring his ignorance of the
matter, Evans said he would speak to the editor,
and then stooped down in search of a paper
containing the offensive article, whereon Goldsmith struck him smartly with his cane across
the back. Jumping up immediately, Evans, a
sturdy man, returned the blow; a scuffle ensued,
during which a lamp suspended overhead was
smashed, and its oil spilled upon the combatants.
One of the shopmen ran for a constable, and
Dr. Kenrick,* who doubtlessly wrote the attack,
rushed from his office, and, separating them, sent
Goldsmith home in a coach. Evans, who received
a black eye, promptly summoned the author for
assault and battery; but friends interfering to
heal the breach, he consented to abandon the
charge, provided Goldsmith gave fifty pounds
towards a charity he mentioned. The doctor com-

---

* Dr. Kenrick was an unsuccessful playwright and an
unpopular man. He has been described in the *Morning
Chronicle* as being "as arrant a snarler as e'er a German
pug in the kingdom."

plying with this demand, the affair was allowed to rest.

The press was unwilling such a topic should quietly subside; various accounts of the affray were given, and in some quarters Goldsmith was condemned for " beating a man in his own house." Therefore he thought it necessary to defend himself, and wrote a forcible letter to the *General Advertiser* of the 31st of March. In this he made no reference to his chastisement of Evans, but, lest it should be supposed he had been willing to correct in others an abuse of which he had been guilty himself, he begged leave to declare in all his life he never wrote or dictated a single paragraph, letter, or essay in a newspaper, except a few moral essays under the character of a Chinese, and a letter, to which he signed his name, in the *St. James's Chronicle.* The press, he said, had turned from defending public interests to making inroads upon private life; from combating the strong to overwhelming the feeble. No condition was too obscure for its abuse, and the protector had become the tyrant of the people.

" How to put a stop to this licentiousness," he

concludes, in a letter presenting one of the finest examples we can boast of vigorous and polished English, "by which all are indiscriminately abused, and by which vice consequently escapes in the general censure, I am unable to tell; all I could wish is that, as the law gives us no protection against the injury, so it should give calumniators no shelter after having provoked correction. The insults which we receive before the public, by being more open are all the more distressing; by treating them with silent contempt we do not pay a sufficient deference to the opinion of the world. By recurring to legal redress we too often expose the weakness of the law, which only serves to increase our mortification by failing to relieve us. In short, every man should singly consider himself as a guardian of the liberty of the press, and, as far as his influence can extend, should endeavour to prevent its licentiousness becoming at last the grave of its freedom."

Twelve months and four days from the date of this letter, the hand that penned it lay cold in death's grasp. Petty jealousy, personal abuse, or bitter criticism would never again disturb poor Goldy's peace.

# RICHARD BRINSLEY SHERIDAN'S RIVALS,

FIRST PRODUCED, 17TH JANUARY, 1775;

AND

## SCHOOL FOR SCANDAL,

FIRST PLAYED, 8TH MAY, 1777.

Bath in the Last Century—The Sheridan Family—Young Dick Sheridan —The Linleys—The Queen Bird—Captain Matthews' Persecutions—Miss Linley Attempts Suicide—Richard's Proposal—Flight and Return— Captain Matthews Seeks Revenge—The Original Bob Acres—Duel by Candle Light—Shame and Humiliation —A Second Encounter—Love's Contrivances—Marriage —She Sang No More—Mrs. Sheridan and Sir Joshua Reynolds—Progress of *The Rivals*—Management of Drury Lane—Sheridan and Garrick—A New Comedy —First Night of *The School for Scandal*—Wonderful Success.

# SHERIDAN'S RIVALS AND SCHOOL FOR SCANDAL.

IN the middle of the last century no gayer city existed within the length and breadth of England than Bath. Beau Nash had not yet risen to originate its Assembly Rooms, frame rules for its manners, and regulate its ways; but men of parts and women of fashion, fatigued by the dissipations and weary of the monotony of London life, crowded here to drink the waters of health and seek fresh means of diversion. In the mornings, gossips of both sexes thronged the Pump Room to slander and calumniate their friends and acquaintance in the smartest and most entertaining manner. At midday, royalty, with its train of courtiers; famous beauties with their groups of followers; belles in powder and patches; beaux in satin and periwigs, wits, flirts, soldiers, and civilians, in all a goodly crowd, took the air in Harrison's Gardens.   When evening came, the narrow streets were filled by the sedans of pleasure-seekers on their way to assemblies, balls, concerts, and card-parties.   The atmosphere of this city of delight was redolent of sin and snuff, rouge and romance, scandal and intrigue; and brilliant with the light of tapers and diamonds, the sheen of silks and swords, the colour of uniforms, and the witchery of women's eyes.

In the year of grace 1770, Thomas Sheridan settled in Bath with his family, one member of which subsequently made the scenes of this pleasant city live in his comedies.   Thomas Sheridan, happily described by Dr. Parr as "a wrong-headed, whimsical man," had pursued a thoroughly active though not wholly profitable career.   Adopting the stage as an occupation, he considered himself superior to David Garrick; becoming manager of a Dublin theatre he lost his fortune; and now following the calling of a public lecturer and teacher of elocution, sought to maintain his family. This consisted of three daughters and two sons— Charles, the eldest, and Richard, the future drama- tist.   Mrs. Sheridan, a writer of novels and plays, had recently died at Blois, in France, a country where the state of her health and the condition of her husband's finances made it desirable for them to reside some time.

Having settled in Bath, Tom Sheridan held classes to "impart the arts of reading and speaking with distinctness and propriety;" in which he was assisted by his eldest and favourite son, who had begun life at the age of twelve as an orator. Richard, born in Dublin in the year 1751, had, from the age of eleven to eighteen, spent his days at Harrow, where he became a general favourite. On leaving school no career had been selected for him by his father, and the lad was accordingly left to follow the bent of his inclinations, and spend his time as he best desired.

He therefore mixed freely among the society which Bath so pleasantly furnished, being "beloved by every one, and greatly respected by all the better sort of people." His sister, describing him at this time, declares he was generally allowed to be handsome; his cheeks had a glow of health, and his eyes were "brilliant with genius, and soft as a tender and affectionate heart could make them." The playful wit, that afterwards distinguished his writings, now cheered and delighted the family circle. " I admired, I almost adored him," she adds enthusiastically.

Amongst the families with whom, on their arrival at Bath, the Sheridans became familiar, were the Linleys. Linley was a musician of fair renown, a conductor of concerts, a composer of note, a man of consequence withal. As was natural, he had bred his children to the calling which had earned him distinction. They have been described by Dr. Burney, in his History of Music, as a family of nightingales, in which the "queen bird" was Elizabeth, Linley's eldest daughter. Before entering her teens she had sung in public, and now took part in oratorios and concerts. Her form was graceful and delicate ; her manners simple and winning; whilst her features, regular and expressive, were touched by that mysterious shadow which prefigures early death. Her bright youth, delicate beauty, and rare talent, rendered her name notable and her company desired. She charmed women by the sweetness of her voice, attracted men by the brightness of her eyes, and was exceedingly lauded by both. Families of rank and fashion contended for her company, and she was received rather as a favourite guest than as a professional singer in the wax-lighted, rose-scented salons of the Parade and the Crescent.

In this bright world, to which she was gladly welcomed, dainty compliments, dangerous flatteries, and luring speeches were whispered in her ear. A score of gallants, wearing their hearts upon their brocaded sleeves, for ever followed in her wake; amongst them being one Captain Matthews, a married man, Elizabeth's senior by many years, a patron of her father's, who under the guise of friendship sought her love. Learned in the arts of a betrayer, he figured before her young imagination as a victim of domestic misery, gaining her sympathy through recounting his woes. For three years he hovered round her, engaging her attention by his studied wiles, whilst blinding her to his ultimate designs.

Towards the end of this time, the Sheridans arrived at Bath, when the two young men, Charles and Richard, immediately fell in love with Miss Linley. In a little while the former proposed to make her his wife; but his offer incurred the displeasure of both families, and was rejected by Elizabeth. Richard behaved with greater caution, and without exciting the suspicions of his elders, gradually gained the girl's confidence, and ultimately won her affection. From the first she found him "agreeable in person, understanding, and accomplishments." She was soon to prove him courageous, honourable, and helpful.

Understanding her past position by the light of her present affection, she was convinced of her error in admitting even a sentimental regard for Matthews, and therefore resolved to sever all communications with him. To this end she was probably advised by Richard Sheridan, who, that he might mentally gauge the captain and render her good service, speedily ingratiated himself into the Lothario's friendship. At first, Sheridan was deceived by him, as Miss Linley subsequently wrote to a friend, "but he soon discovered the depravity of his heart under the specious appearance of virtue which he at times assumed, and resolved to make use of a little art to endeavour, if he could, to save me from such a villain. For this purpose he disguised his real sentiments and became the most intimate friend of Matthews, who at last entrusted him with all his designs in regard to me, and boasted to him how cleverly he had deceived me, for that I believed him an angel."

Escape from the clutches of such a man was a task more difficult of accomplishment than Miss Linley anticipated ; moreover, in her efforts to elude him, she was unassisted by her parents. Dreading the results of her father's violent temper, she withheld from him all knowledge of Matthews' particular attentions, but revealed them to her mother, who laughed at what she considered romantic fancies, and declared the girl thought every man who paid her a compliment must be in love with her. Matthews' intimacy with the family, and his private addresses to Miss Linley, were therefore continued.

At this period of her history an elderly gentleman, named Richard Walter Long, the owner of vast estates in Wiltshire, fell in love with, and proposed to marry her. Because of his wealth and station his suit was favourably regarded by her parents, who strenuously insisted she should accept so excellent an offer. In obedience to their hard commands she was therefore engaged to Mr. Long ; who, in accordance with a stipulation made by Linley, agreed to pay a thousand pounds by way of indemnification for the loss Miss Linley's retirement from public life would occasion her family. Meanwhile, as the day appointed for her union with Long approached, the girl's wretchedness increased; until, at last gaining courage from desperation, she, possibly at the suggestion of young Sheridan, flung herself upon the generosity of her elderly suitor, and, declaring her marriage with him would result in greatest misery, besought release from her engagement. The old gentleman behaved with the utmost chivalry, and not only acceded to her request, but took upon himself the blame of breaking their engagement. Learning the plight had been broken, Linley threatened an action for breach of promise of marriage, when Long generously settled three thousand pounds as a dowry upon the woman he loved.

The excitement these circumstances produced, acting on a nervous organisation, caused Elizabeth Linley serious illness, which it was feared might develop into consumption; a condition Captain Matthews attributed to his powers of fascination over an unsatisfied heart. Charles Sheridan, on the other hand, imagining her engagement to have been abandoned because of her secret love for him, again proposed, and was once more rejected. Grievously disappointed, he betook himself for some weeks into the country, and therefore, was absent from Bath, when the most important scenes in the drama of Elizabeth Linley's life were enacted. Meanwhile Richard, yet keeping his affection hidden from all, not only saw her continually in public, but occasionally contrived to meet her in private; their trysting-place being " a moss-covered grotto of stone, shaded by dew-dropping willows." In this shrine of romance, situated in Sydney Gardens, the lovers whispered long of troubles surrounding them as a sombre sea, from which they saw no means of escape; for he having neither money, profession, nor prospects, and she being followed by ardent admirers and subject to the wishes of mercenary parents, there seemed small chance of their ultimate union.

The while, gossip was busy with her name. In the Pump Room during the morning, on the Parade in the afternoon, and at polite assemblies in the evening, the principal topic of conversation was Miss Linley and her admirers. And Linley, now becoming aware of reports linking his daughter's name with Matthews', and growing fearful of its consequences, severed all friendly intercourse with him, and made her promise she would see the captain no more. With this request Elizabeth was most willing to comply, and, writing to acquaint Matthews with her father's decision, begged they might part as friends; whereon he commissioned Richard Sheridan to assure Linley he would avoid seeing his daughter in future.

For a while all went well, until one day Matthews privately wrote to her declaring he was going to London for two months, and if she refused to see him on his return, he would certainly shoot himself. Elizabeth answered, commenting on the injustice of his conduct, and requesting he would not again address her. To this she received a reply stating he had something to communicate of the utmost importance to her happiness, and begging she would grant him a few minutes' conversation. If this were denied, he added, she might expect to hear of fatal consequences. Terrified by threats she agreed to his proposal, and met him at the house of a mutual friend; when, producing a pistol, he swore, if she did not promise to grant him another interview, he would shoot himself before her face. Distraught with excitement and trembling with terror she pledged her word, and then, bidding her meet him four days later, he released her. Before reaching home she resolved on escaping from his persecutions by destroying her life, and to accomplish this purpose secretly procured laudanum.

The following day being Sunday she attended church with her mother and sisters, but, refusing to accompany them on a walk, returned home, made her will, and wrote farewell letters to her father and Captain Matthews. Whilst engaged in this manner Richard Sheridan entered the room, and, seeing the laudanum and the letters, suspected her intention. He therefore sought to persuade her from such designs, and, being unsuccessful, made her promise to postpone their execution till the afternoon, when he might have news that would change her resolution. No sooner, however, had he departed than, fearful of betrayal, she drank the laudanum, and was soon after found in a condition at first mistaken for death.

A distressing scene followed. Her parents were overwhelmed by grief and remorse, her sisters heartbroken and distracted. The doctors, how-

ever, had hope of restoring her, and on the evening of the following day she was sufficiently
recovered to see Sheridan, who now revealed
Matthews's true character, showing her for the
purpose several letters he had from time to time
received from the captain. In one of these it
was stated Miss Linley had given him so much
trouble, that he would renounce all pursuit of
her if his vanity did not desire conquest. He
was resolved, therefore, when they met on Wednesday, to abandon the character of a suppliant
and to assume the authority of a master. But
if she refused to meet him, he would carry her
away by force. Having read this letter she
fainted. On recovery Sheridan asked her what
plans suggested themselves to her for protection.
" I told him," she said, " my mind was in such
a state of distraction between anger, remorse,
and fear, that I did not know what I should do ;
but as Matthews had declared he would ruin my
reputation, I was resolved never to stay in Bath."

Sheridan then proposed she should fly with
him to France, where he would place her in a
convent in which his sisters had been educated.
Here she would be safe from danger, and, when

he had seen her settled, he "would return to England and place her conduct in such a light that
the world would applaud and not condemn her."
This being a period when violence and abduction
were common occurrences, she evidently had little
faith in the protection her father could extend
against the arts of a man of wealth and position.
Therefore, consenting to Sheridan's plans, she
agreed to be guided by him entirely. Accordingly
he made secret preparations for their departure,
in which he was aided by his eldest sister, who,
favouring the scheme, helped him with such money
as she could spare from the household expenses.

At last the time fixed for departure—the
evening of the day on which Elizabeth Linley
had promised to meet Matthews—arrived. The
hour had been well selected by the lovers. Her
mother lay ill in bed, her father, brother, and
sisters were performing at a concert, from which
she had absented herself on plea of indisposition.

. All things being arranged, Sheridan, unheeded
in the gathering dusk, arrived at the Crescent
followed by two sedan chairs. Into one he handed
Miss Linley, in the other he placed her luggage.
Then, bidding the carriers proceed to the London

Road, he walked behind by way of protection. He had not followed many yards when he encountered Matthews, who, furious Miss Linley had not kept her appointment, was about calling at her mother's house. Sheridan assured him of Mrs. Linley's illness, and, stating he was engaged in an affair of honour, in which he might require assistance, begged Matthews would await him at his sister's. The captain complying, Sheridan followed the chairs until they arrived at the London Road. Here a post-chaise stood waiting, in which Miss Linley found an elderly married woman, whom Sheridan had engaged to accompany them as a duenna. The lovers then drove in all haste to London, which they reached that night.

Arriving in town, Sheridan sought an old friend of his father's, one Ewart, a brandy merchant in the city. By way of gaining Ewart's assistance in his undertaking, Sheridan introduced Miss Linley as a wealthy heiress, who had consented to elope with him to the continent. Rejoiced at the young man's good fortune the old gentleman bade him heartily welcome, congratulated him on his undertaking, and offered him every possible assistance. As luck ordained, a vessel, chartered by Ewart, was then ready to sail for Dunkirk, in which he willingly gave them passage, and moreover presented them with letters of introduction to his partners there, whom he besought to facilitate their departure for Lille. On arriving at Dunkirk, the fugitives, in order to silence any scandal that might arise, went through a ceremony of marriage, performed by a Catholic priest. They then set out for Lille. Here Sheridan took an apartment in a convent for his companion, where she was to remain whilst he returned to England and prepared their future home.

She had not been many days at the convent when, overcome by fatigue and weakened by excitement, she became seriously ill. Sheridan therefore postponed his homeward journey and sought advice from an English physician, Dr. Dolman, of York, who, with his wife, was then staying at Lille. These kindly people betrayed the friendliest interest in the invalid ; and, believing she would feel more comfortable in their home, invited her to stay there whilst her indisposition lasted. Sheridan and his wife—as she may be called— had written to Linley, from whom they agreed to conceal their marriage, simply stating this step had been undertaken to save her from peril and perhaps ruin.

To these letters no answers were returned. A missive, however, reached Sheridan from Matthews, who from the hour of Miss Linley's departure had persecuted the members of her family with inquiries for the fugitives. From them he had obtained Sheridan's address, and used it to threaten and abuse the man who had baulked him in his evil designs. To his offensive epistle Sheridan replied he would return immediately, and would never sleep a night in England until he had thanked him as he deserved. Meanwhile Matthews, by way of avenging himself, inserted the following paragraphs in the *Bath Chronicle* of Wednesday, April 8, 1772 :

"Mr. Richard S—— having attempted, in a letter left behind him for that purpose, to account for his scandalous method of running away from this place, by insinuations derogating from my character and that of a young lady, innocent as far as relates to me, or my knowledge ; since which he has neither taken any notice of letters, nor even informed his own family of the place where he has hid himself ; I can no longer think he deserves the treatment of a gentleman, and therefore shall trouble myself no further about him than, in this public method, to post him as a l—— and a treacherous s——.

"And as I am convinced there have been many malevolent incendiaries concerned in the propagation of this infamous lie, if any of them, unprotected by age, infirmities, or profession, will dare to acknowledge the part they have acted and affirm to what they have said of me, they may depend on receiving the proper reward of their villainy in the most public manner. The world will be candid enough to judge properly (I make no doubt) of any private abuse on this subject for the future, as nobody can defend himself from an accusation he is ignorant of.

"THOMAS MATTHEWS."


Sheridan, though unaware of this public attack, was anxious to hurry home that he might punish Matthews for his private insolence, but before he departed Linley arrived. Thoroughly satisfied with the explanations Sheridan gave, he thanked him for the protection afforded his daughter, whom he heartily pardoned. However, he insisted she should return immediately, in order to fulfil some professional engagements he had made on her behalf; after which, he said, she might return to the protection of the convent if she pleased.

Therefore they three set out for London, and, on arriving, sought hospitality of good Mr. Ewart. On their way from Dover they had stayed a night at Canterbury, where Sheridan refused to seek rest, that he might keep his promise of not sleeping in England before meeting his slanderer. Hearing the latter was in town, Sheridan, on reaching London, immediately went in search of him, but it was late at night before he discovered the captain was located at a lodging-house in Crutched Friars. Arriving here towards midnight and knocking loudly, Matthews came down, but, recognising his visitor's voice, declared the key of the door was lost, and promising Sheridan should be admitted when it was found, promptly retired to bed. This excuse did not suffice to divert Sheridan from his purpose; he persisted in knocking at the door and alarming the neighbourhood until two o'clock in the morning, when he was admitted. He then made his way to Matthews' room, when the latter arose, complained of cold, called Sheridan his dear friend, and begged he would be seated. His whole bearing was that of a coward, who, seeing the hour of his punishment had arrived, sought escape by protestations of civility.

Sheridan said he had come to answer his challenge, when Matthews declared he had never meant to quarrel; that his dear friend's anger should be vented on his brother Charles, who, enraged by Miss Linley's preference, had prompted him to write the note. Blinded by rage on hearing this, Richard hastened to Bath, and, seeking Charles, demanded an explanation. High words passed between them, which resulted in both hastening back by post-chaise to town in order to punish Matthews, not only for his slander but for his last lie. Richard immediately called him out, and, accompanied by young Ewart, met Matthews and his second, Captain Knight, in Hyde Park. Coming to the ring, Sheridan observed this was their ground; but Matthews—doubtless the original Bob Acres—objected to the spot. Therefore proceeding some yards they arrived at a level space, when Sheridan paused again, but his unwilling antagonist declared the

place too public. They agreed to wait until the
Park was deserted, and, after a considerable time,
Sheridan once more prepared for combat. But
the gallant captain, perceiving a solitary figure
in the distance, roundly swore they were watched,
and, protesting he would not fight whilst any
one was in sight, suggested the duel should be
postponed until morning.

This Sheridan declared to be mere trifling;
however, that Matthews might have no excuse,
he went forward and requested the figure to with-
draw. On his return he discerned Matthews
quickly making his way out of the Park, when
he immediately followed, and, swearing he
should fight, conducted him to the Castle
Tavern in Henrietta Street, Covent Garden.
Here Ewart called for lights, and led the party
to a private room, when they drew their swords.
The contest was sharp and brief; in a few seconds
Sheridan's opponent was at his mercy, whereon Captain Knight rushed forward crying, " Don't
kill him !" and Matthews begged for his life.
The victor then broke his opponent's sword, and
insisted he should write a contradiction of the

statements falsely made. With this he refused compliance, but Sheridan declaring he should not leave the room until this satisfaction had been rendered him, Captain Matthews was obliged to write the following lines at Richard Sheridan's dictation :

"Being convinced that the expressions I made use of to Mr. Sheridan's disadvantage were the effects of passion and misrepresentation, I retract what I have said to that gentleman's disadvantage, and particularly beg his pardon for my advertisement in the *Bath Chronicle.*

"THOMAS MATTHEWS."

The Sheridans, returning to Bath, caused this apology to be inserted in the paper which had originally published the accusation. In recounting the incidents of their duel Richard generously refrained from observations contrary to his adversary's credit ; chance, he said, had given him advantage in the affair, and Matthews had therefore written his apology. Two days later the gallant captain arrived, and represented the encounter in a manner casting insinuations on his

P

antagonist's behaviour whilst extolling his own
bravery; hearing which Sheridan made known
the truth.    Accordingly the story of Matthews'
cowardice, spreading through Bath, caused him
to be shunned by men and ridiculed by women.
He therefore hastily retreated to his home in
Wales, but the news of his conduct having
arrived before him, he was there likewise slighted
and derided by friends and neighbours.

Stung by repeated mortifications, he sought
to retrieve his honour by the desperate expedient
of fighting a second duel with his late antagonist.    For this purpose he returned to Bath,
accompanied by one Barnett, on whom he greatly
depended to sustain his courage, and challenged
Sheridan to combat.    The latter, having already
avenged his injuries and given ample proofs of
his courage, was at liberty to decline the meeting
without blemish to his honour; but, impetuous
and heroic, he accepted it with alacrity.    The
bitter slights under which Matthews writhed had
wrought his spirit to the highest pitch, and he
determined the second duel should prove fatal
to one or other of the combatants.

Of this Sheridan was well aware, and now it was his fate to be parted from those dearest to him. His wife was fulfilling an engagement at Oxford, his father and brother were absent in London. The day fixed for the duel at last arrived, and on the morning of the 1st July, 1772, he and his second, Captain Paumier, met Matthews and his supporter at Kingsdown, about four miles outside Bath. It was but three o'clock. Night had scarce faded from the fields, and the profound silence brooding over the mystery of dawn was unbroken, when they left their respective chaises and sought the ground already selected for their encounter. Here they at once drew their swords. Sheridan rapidly advanced on his opponent, then gradually retreated, and finally running in on Matthews sought to catch his sword. In this he failed, when the captain dealt him a blow which broke his weapon. He then laid hold of Sheridan's sword-arm, and tripping him suddenly, both came to the ground. Matthews, being uppermost, seized his broken sword and repeatedly struck his fallen foe on the neck and face. Neither of the seconds interfered. Sheridan's sword had been bent in the fall, but, managing to grasp its point, he succeeded in wounding his antagonist slightly in the stomach; the latter then seized the point of his sword and stabbed Sheridan repeatedly. Both were furious from passion, maddened by pain, and covered with blood. Matthews now called out: "Beg your life, and I will be yours for ever!" and this request was repeated by Barnett; but Sheridan fiercely cried out, with an oath, he would never ask mercy. The seconds now interfered to part them, but before this act could be achieved Matthews declared Sheridan should be disarmed; and this being accomplished they were conveyed to separate chaises waiting close by, when Matthews, who was but slightly wounded, drove to London, and Sheridan was carried to the White Hart Tavern, where two of the most famous physicians in Bath were speedily summoned to his aid.

At the request of his sisters he was conveyed to their father's house the following day, and for a week continued in extreme danger. Meanwhile alarming reports of the duel and its consequences appeared in various papers, one of which reached

Linley at Oxford as he was about to conduct an oratorio. He managed, however, to conceal the news from his daughter, knowing it would prevent her singing. Presently the family set out for Bath, and arriving within a few miles from town were met by the Rev. Mr. Panton, who entering into conversation with Miss Linley, begged she would undertake the remainder of the journey in his chaise. He then with due preparation told her of the duel, on which, overcome by surprise, she cried out, "My husband, my husband!" and begged she might be taken to him. Compliance with this request was, however, impossible, as Sheridan's father now forbade his family to hold intercourse with the Linleys, whom he blamed as the cause of his son's folly; whilst her parents were equally anxious she should avoid young Sheridan.

When pronounced out of danger, Richard was sent to visit some friends at Waltham that he might recover strength, whilst his wife was placed under care of relatives at Tunbridge Wells. On their return to Bath the utmost caution was taken by the Linleys that Sheridan should not see their eldest daughter ; and so carefully was she guarded, that for long she found it impossible to write him a letter or receive one from him. At length he conceived a stratagem which out-witted vigilance. Arriving at an understanding with the owner of vehicles hired to convey her to concerts, he disguised himself as their driver, when he dexterously slipped notes into her palm, and received others in return as he handed her out. In this way their vows of fidelity were renewed, until at length perseverance was re-warded, opposition relented, and they were married on the 13th of April, 1773, the bride-groom being twenty-two years and the bride nineteen.

So much has been recorded of Sheridan's early life, because of the influence it subsequently bore upon his productions, many scenes of which reflect incidents and characters which had come within his personal experience.

A few months previous to his marriage Sheridan had been entered as a student of the Middle Temple, but now neither time nor money necessary to the pursuit of his profession was at his disposal. His father had declined to countenance his union, and refused him future help; and Richard, scorning to make use of his wife's talents for their common support, had determinedly rejected profitable engagements offered her.* His objections to her continuing a professional singer were exceedingly strong. She having before their marriage made an agreement to sing at the Worcester Musical Meeting, Sheridan, after great pressure from the directors,

* In this determination, which satisfied his pride and saved her from continual temptations, he earned the approval of Dr. Johnson. "We talked," says Boswell, "of a young gentleman's marriage with an eminent singer, and his determination that she should no longer sing in public, though his father was very earnest she should, because her talents would be liberally rewarded, so as to make her a good fortune. It was questioned whether the young gentleman, who had not a shilling in the world, but was blest with very uncommon talents, was not foolishly delicate, or foolishly proud, and his father truly rational, without being mean. Johnson, with all the high spirit of a Roman senator, exclaimed: 'He resolved wisely and nobly, to be sure. He is a brave man. Would not a gentleman be disgraced by having his wife sing publicly for hire? No, sir, there can be no doubt here. I know not if I should not prepare myself for a public singer as readily as let my wife be one.'" The happy change in public opinion since this sentence was delivered, is worthy of note.

permitted her to fulfil her promise, but gave her salary to public charities; and once more he allowed her to sing at the ceremony of Lord North's installation as Chancellor of Oxford, "merely to oblige his Lordship and the University." Nay, so anxious was he her profession should be forgotten, that he discouraged exhibitions of her talent in private assemblies. Northcote records how Sir Joshua Reynolds invited the Sheridans, soon after their marriage, to one of his famous dinners, together with a large number of guests, in hopes she would gratify them by her singing. That she might have a suitable accompaniment he hired a full-toned piano. But, to his great mortification, "on hints being given that a song from her would be received as a gratification and favour, Mr. Sheridan answered that Mrs. Sheridan, with his assent, had come to a resolution never again to sing in company. Sir Joshua repeated this next day," says Northcote, "in my hearing with some degree of anger, saying, 'What reason could they think I had to invite them to dinner, unless it was to hear her sing, for she cannot talk?'"

The young couple began life on part of the

fortune settled on Mrs. Sheridan by Long. Meanwhile, her husband strove to earn an income by writing for journals and magazines, in which occupation he was occasionally aided by his wife, who had given proof of her literary talent by turning sentimental verses and inditing pretty letters. " We are obliged," he told one of his friends, "to write for our daily leg of mutton, otherwise we should have no dinner."

"Ah!" replied his confidant, " I perceive it is a joint affair."

In the year succeeding his marriage he was engaged on a book, of which no trace has been discovered, and on a comedy subsequently known as *The Rivals.* " I have done it," he says, writing of the play to his father-in-law, " at Mr. Harris's (the manager's) own request; it is now complete in his hands and preparing for the stage. He, and some of his friends also who have heard it, assure me in the most flattering terms that there is not a doubt of its success. It will be very well played, and Harris tells me that the least shilling I shall get—if it succeeds—will be six hundred pounds. I shall make no secret of it towards the time of representation, that it may not lose any support my friends can give it. I had not written a line of it two months ago, except a scene or two, which I believe you have seen in an odd act of a little farce."

*The Rivals* was first produced on the 17th of January, 1775, Shuter, Woodward, Lewes, Quick, and Lee, respectively playing the parts of Sir Anthony Absolute, Captain Absolute, Falkland, Bob Acres, and Sir Lucius O'Trigger. John Bernard, an actor of repute and experience, has, in his Retrospection of the Stage, given his impressions of the first night's representation. " It was so intolerably long, and so decidedly opposed in its composition to the taste of the day," he writes, " as to draw down a degree of censure, which convinced me on quitting the house that it would never succeed. It must be remembered that this was the English 'age of sentiment,' and that Cumberland and Hugh Kelly had flooded the stage with moral poems under the title of comedies, which took their views of life from the drawing-room exclusively, and coloured their characters with a nauseous French affectation. *The Rivals*, in my opinion, was a decided attempt to overthrow this taste, and follow up the blow which Goldsmith had given in *She Stoops to Conquer*. My recollection of the manner in which the former was received bears me out in the supposition. The audience on this occasion were composed of two parties—those who supported the prevailing taste, and those who were indifferent to it, and liked nature. On the first night of a new play it was very natural that the former should predominate ; and what was the consequence? why, that Falkland and Julia—which Sheridan had obviously introduced to conciliate the sentimentalists, but which in the present day are considered heavy incumbrances—were the characters which were most favourably received, whilst Sir Anthony, Acres, and Lydia, those faithful and diversified pictures of life, were barely tolerated, and Mrs. Malaprop was singled out for peculiar vengeance."

After its second representation the comedy was withdrawn. Its failure was chiefly attributed to the bad acting of Lee as Sir Lucius. His part having been given to Clinch, and some alterations effected in the dialogue, it was again performed, and gradually rose into favour with the town.

Towards the end of the year 1775, Sheridan

produced a comic opera entitled *The Duenna*, a light, brilliant offspring of his genius, plentifully interspersed with sprightly airs by Linley, one of which at least, " Had I a heart for falsehood framed," is not wholly unknown to the present generation. *The Duenna* became immediately popular, and succeeded in running twelve nights longer than *The Beggar's Opera*. Fortune indeed now smiled on Sheridan, for before another year had passed he, at the age of twenty-five, became part manager and proprietor of Drury Lane Theatre.

This important step had been brought about by Garrick, who, having achieved fame such as no actor had previously earned, and accumulated fortune proportionate to his success, resolved on retiring from the stage, withdrawing from management, and selling his moiety in the patent of Drury Lane playhouse. Rumour of this intention having spread through town, Garrick was beset by numbers anxious to purchase his share, amounting to thirty-five thousand pounds ; but the manager, having first tendered it to Colman, of Covent Garden, next offered it to Sheridan, who, in conjunction with Linley and Dr. Ford, was desirous of acquiring the property. The sum

of thirty-five thousand pounds was considerable
to the future shareholders ; " but, I think," writes
the young dramatist to his father-in-law, " we
might safely give five thousand pounds more on
this purchase than richer people. The whole is
valued at seventy thousand pounds ; the annual'
interest is three thousand five hundred ; while
this is cleared the proprietors are safe, but I think
it must be infernal management indeed that does
not double it." And again, he hopefully tells
Linley, " I'll answer for it we shall see many
golden campaigns."

In June, 1776, the sale of Garrick's share was
duly effected. Sheridan and Linley paid ten
thousand pounds each, Dr. Ford fifteen thousand
pounds, and the brilliant young playwright in a
little while became directing manager. Lacy,
who had been Garrick's partner, and still held
his share of thirty-five thousand pounds, was in
Sheridan's estimation " utterly unequal to any department in the theatre. He has an opinion of
me," he continues, " and is very willing to let
the whole burden and responsibility be taken off
his shoulders. But I certainly should not give
up my time and labour—for his superior advan-

tage, having so much greater a share—without some exclusive advantage. Yet I should by no means make the demand till I had shown myself equal to the task."

In February, 1777, the new manager produced a comedy, *A Trip to Scarborough*, which was merely an alteration from *The Relapse*, by Vanbrugh, and then set to work in writing *The School for Scandal*. The composition of this famous play, apparently the issue of happy chance and unpremeditated wit, was emphatically the result of serious thought and untiring industry. Two distinct sketches of the comedy were first made, which, after consideration and trial, developed into one perfect whole. In the first outline, Lady Sneerwell and her slanderous associates, her ward Maria, and a sentimental young gentleman named Clerimont, are the chief characters; in the second, Oliver Teazle, a retired merchant, his wife, and Plausible and Pliable —the originals of Joseph and Charles Surface—are the principal personages. The sparkling repartee of the first, and the motive of the second, combined to present the most brilliant picture of eighteenth-century society known to the stage.

Evidence remains, in his manuscripts, of the

care Sheridan devoted in constructing his sentences, of the labour he underwent in displaying
his humour to the best advantage. Repeatedly
he expressed one idea in various forms, by way
of ascertaining its most effective use ; and he continually refined his wit till it shone with brighter
lustre in each new setting. And, as he toiled,
so did he triumph. Involved meanings, over-
glaring witticisms, cumbrous sentences, were sim-
plified, softened, and curtailed, as he proceeded.
The time occupied in polishing the comedy was
greater than he had anticipated, and, the piece
being announced for performance before it was
finished, the last scenes were roughly scribbled
on detached pieces of paper. Towards the close,
his work evidently became irksome to its author,
who, arriving at a conclusion, wrote after the
final words : " Finished at last. Thank God.
R. B. Sheridan." To which the prompter, no
less grateful, added : "Amen. A. Hopkins."

The comedy being advertised, the town awaited
its representation with interest. Garrick had di-
verted his elegant leisure by reading it with close
attention, and, as Arthur Murphy records, had
spoken of it with the highest approbation in all

companies, a compliment the author fully appreciated. Between them a kindly friendship had been established. Tom Davies says Sheridan esteemed and loved Garrick, "knew the value of his advice, and implicitly relied upon his experience and discernment." On the other hand, the great actor paid Sheridan the loftiest compliment possible by placing him on a mental level with himself; for, when one of Garrick's admirers regretted the Atlas who had long propped the stage, had left his station, the late manager replied, "If that be the case he has found another young Hercules to fulfil the office."

Anxious for Sheridan's success Garrick daily attended the rehearsals, to which he brought the benefit of his exact judgment and skilled experience. Moreover, he wrote a long prologue for the comedy, a form of composition in which he excelled. The newspaper advertisements announced the play as "never before performed," but made no mention of the author's name; and the preliminary notices declared the comedy "would be ornamented with scenes which did honour to the painters, and furnished with dresses new and elegant."

At length the evening of May 8th, 1777, the date fixed for first performance of the comedy, arrived. The doors of Drury Lane playhouse opened at half-past five o'clock, and, before an hour passed, "a brilliant and crowded audience," to borrow a phrase from the *Public Advertiser*, had assembled. In due time, the curtain rising, King came forward to speak Garrick's prologue, which, with much pleasantry, "adverted to the title of the comedy and shot an arrow of pointed satire at the too general proneness to detraction observable in the daily and evening papers." Then the comedy began, and a play of wit, exchange of repartee, and charm of diction flashed on the hearers with surprise and delight. " The loudest testimonies of applause," the London *Evening Post* of the following day states, "greeted the comedy between every act ; " and the *Daily Advertiser* adds : " it was received with the highest marks of universal approbation." The full force of enthusiastic approval was reserved for the screen scene in the fourth act, which, according to the *Public Advertiser*, " produced a burst of applause beyond anything ever heard perhaps in a theatre." A further testimony of the sensation this scene caused is recorded by Frederick Reynolds, the dramatist, in his Life and Times. On this night he was returning from Lincoln's Inn about nine o'clock, "and passing through the pit passage from Vinegar Yard to Brydges Street," he writes, " I heard such a tremendous noise over my head, that, fearing the theatre was proceeding to fall about it, I ran for my life, but found the next morning that the noise did not arise from the falling of the house, but from the falling of the screen in the fourth act, so violent and so tumultuous were the applause and laughter."

The following players sustained the original cast :

| | |
|---|---|
| Sir Peter Teazle . . . . | MR. KING. |
| Sir Oliver Surface . . . | MR. YATES. |
| Sir Harry Bumper . . . | MR. GAWDRY. |
| Sir Benjamin Backbite . . | MR. DODD. |
| Joseph Surface . . . . | MR. PALMER. |
| Charles Surface . . . . | MR. SMITH. |
| Careless . . . . . | MR. FARREN. |
| Snake . . . . . . | MR. PACKER. |
| Crabtree . . . . . | MR. PARSONS. |
| Rowley . . . . . | MR. AICKIN. |
| Moses . . . . . . | MR. BADDELEY. |
| Trip . . . . . . | MR. LAMASH. |
| Lady Teazle . . . . | MRS. ABINGTON. |
| Lady Sneerwell . . . . | MISS SHERRY. |
| Mrs. Candour . . . . | MISS POPE. |
| Maria . . . . . | MISS P. HOPKINS. |

Owing to frequent rehearsals, and the care exercised by Sheridan, the performance on this night was unusually good, and largely helped to secure success for the play. Mrs. Abington, as Lady Teazle, exhibited grace and vivacity. Smith's playing of Charles Surface, and King's representation of Sir Peter Teazle, were pronounced admirable. The remainder of the company were almost equally excellent. " To my great surprise," writes Horace Walpole, who witnessed it some nights later, " there were more parts performed admirably in this comedy than I almost ever saw in any play. Mrs. Abington was equal to the first in her profession; Yates, Parsons, Miss Pope, and Palmer all shone."

The curtain fell, at the close of the first performance, on a scene of enthusiasm such as the walls of old Drury had seldom witnessed, and, before morning dawned, the happy playwright, then in his twenty-sixth year, was, as he told Lord Byron many years later, " knocked down, and put into the watch-house, for making a row in the street and being found intoxicated by the watchmen." Next day the London press expressed its admiration of the brilliant comedy.

The *Public Advertiser* was of opinion Sheridan had united in one piece the easy dialogue of Cibber, the humour and truth of Vanbrugh, with the refined wit and pleasantry of Congreve. The *Gazetteer* pronounced his genius "had happily restored the English drama to those rays of glory of which it was being shorn by a tedious set of contemptible scribblers." The *Morning Chronicle* declared the dialogue of his comedy to be "easy, engaging, and witty, abounding in strokes of pointed satire and enriched by a vein of humour pervading the whole." The objections it pointed out were that the production was somewhat too long, the scandal scenes were overcharged, and the last act was hastily composed. The *Morning Post* alone hit the sole blemish of this well-nigh faultless play. "If," says this journal, "there is a part that the pen of criticism can justly point out as exceptionable, it will be found in the second act, where, in our opinion, the business of the piece is suffered to hang in compliment to a chain of wit traps, some of which seem rather too studiously laid to have the desired effect."

Sheridan had now secured the reputation of having written the most brilliant comedy in our language. He has since earned the gratitude of countless numbers for the gratification it has afforded them. Its success continued at full tide during the remainder of the season, and was received with renewed enthusiasm the following autumn. Indeed, its continued representation for the next two years, whilst powerless to lessen its own popularity, was detrimental to the success of later productions, as may be surmised from the following remark, written by the treasurer of Drury Lane in his official report of the receipts for 1789 : " *School for Scandal* damped the new pieces."

Before this date it was played in Dublin, Edinburgh, Bath, and many of the larger towns in England, and was everywhere received with hearty approbation. In 1788 the screen and auction scenes were embodied in a piece called *Les Deux Neveux*, played with success in Paris, and later on it was produced at the Théâtre Français, under the title *Le Tartuffe des Mœurs*, and at the Porte St. Martin as *L'École du*

*Scandale.* A version of the comedy was produced in Vienna by Schröder, an actor and author of repute, who travelled to England for the purpose of seeing it performed; and it has also been played in the Hague.

It was not until some years after Sheridan's death, one of his biographers ventured to insinuate the comedy had been pirated from a nameless young lady, the daughter of a merchant in Thames Street, who, obligingly dying of consumption, left Sheridan in possession of her manuscripts. "While time rolls on," says Dr. Watkins, in a fine spirit of false prophecy, "the difficulty of settling this question must necessarily be increasing, and this, in all probability, will be one of those critical points about which the spirit of literary research will labour in vain." The ball which this foolish doctor of laws sought to set rolling was timely stopped. Even if *The Rivals*, *The Duenna*, and later on *The Critic*, did not claim *The School for Scandal* as kindred, Sheridan's original sketches of the comedy happily remained to prove the worthlessness of this ingenious aspersion.

# SHERIDAN KNOWLES'
# VIRGINIUS,

## FIRST PRODUCED, 17TH MAY, 1820;

### AND

# THE HUNCHBACK,

## FIRST PLAYED, 5TH APRIL, 1832.

A Clever Boy—Some Famous Friends—In the Militia—
Becomes a Doctor—Passion for the Stage—A Provincial
Player—With Edmund Kean—Abandons the Stage—
Play-writing and Its Profits—A Schoolmaster's Life—
Various Struggles — Writing *The Hunchback* — The
Kembles at Drury Lane—Success of *The Hunchback*—
Fanny Kemble Says Farewell—Knowles as an Actor.

# JAMES SHERIDAN KNOWLES' VIRGINIUS AND THE HUNCHBACK.

JAMES SHERIDAN KNOWLES was born on the 12th of May, 1784, in Cork. His father, James Knowles, was nephew to Thomas Sheridan, and first cousin to the author of *The School for Scandal*. For upwards of twelve years James Knowles was master of a prosperous academy in the southern capital of Ireland. Towards the end of that period he quarrelled with his patrons regarding political opinions, when, the number of his pupils gradually diminishing, he was obliged to seek his fortunes elsewhere. At this time the future dramatist, James Sheridan Knowles, was in his ninth year. In youth he gave promise of the talents which distinguished his maturity. Before reaching the age of thirteen he wrote a drama, which he and his companions acted in his mother's drawing-room; and two years later he composed " The Welsh Harper," a ballad that subsequently became exceedingly popular.

His intellectual gifts received no encouragement from his father, a pedantic, pompous little schoolmaster, who sported a gold-rimmed eye-glass and lived to write a dictionary; but were fostered by the appreciation of his mother and the praise of his friends, amongst whom he reckoned William Hazlitt, Charles Lamb, and Samuel Coleridge. These three distinguished men treated him with kindness. Hazlitt, then a struggling artist, painted his portrait; Lamb criticised his efforts; and Coleridge lectured him on poetry. Before he was sixteen a crisis came in his life. His mother, who had been his literary confidant and trusted friend, died, and James Knowles shortly afterwards married again. In consequence of this change the lad soon became aware his father's house was no longer his home; therefore, leaving it in indignation, he sought independence. In maintaining this resolution he was aided by his cousin Richard Brinsley Sheridan, who obtained a place for him in the Stamp Office.

Subsequently Sheridan Knowles served as ensign in the Wiltshire Militia, from which he was transferred to the Second Tower Hamlets. At this time an incident happened in his life savouring more of romance than reality. Dr. Willan, a benevolent old gentleman who had realised a considerable fortune, and enjoyed an extensive practice, taking a fancy to the young ensign, conceived the idea of adopting him as his son, and training him for the medical profession, that he might eventually succeed him. For a while Sheridan Knowles hesitated to accept this generous offer, having no vocation for the study of medicine, and fearing his obligations might hamper his independence. However, conscious of the benefits it promised, and urged by the solicitations of friends, he eventually accepted Dr. Willan's proposal with gratitude.

He therefore read, studied, and visited patients under the guidance of his patron ; and vaccination being introduced at this period, he became one of its earliest supporters and most earnest advocates. Presently the Jennerian Society contemplating the appointment of a resident vaccinator, Knowles obtained the post through influence of Dr. Willan, who likewise procured him a degree of Doctor of Medicine from the Aberdeen University.

Before he had reached his twenty-fifth year he was established resident inoculator to the Jennerian Society, at a salary of two hundred pounds a year, with a house in Salisbury Square. Working with ardour in his new pursuit, he was instrumental in abating the scourge of small-pox and rescuing many lives. But the enthusiasm with which he laboured never blinded him to his unsuitability for the profession he had adopted. Instead of possessing the sober disposition becoming a physician, Sheridan Knowles had the temperament of an artist. His jaunty step, careless air, and smiling face lacked the gravity, concentrativeness, and reserve becoming a medical man. Nor was his heart in the work he performed. The drama was seldom absent from his thoughts in leisure hours, and, notwithstanding his busy life, he found time to write, and take part in, a five-act tragedy called *The Spanish Story*. Fired by the commendation bestowed on this composition, he promptly resolved to abandon a profession never congenial to his taste, and to follow a calling which apparently promised renown. He was wise enough to understand that, before writing for the stage, he must obtain practical knowledge of its requirements; therefore he resolved to become an actor. He immediately communicated his determination and ambition to his generous friend, Dr. Willan. "I wish to be independent," he said. "I will write for the stage, and make a name and fortune for myself. I will go to the provinces and practise, and, when I am fit for a London audience, I will come back to you. Some worthy fellow will be the better for the position which I have held so long, and for which I have no liking, though I have tried to gratify you."

Good Dr. Willan was distressed at this resolve, but believed his pupil's love for the stage merely a passing fancy. "Farewell, my boy," he is recorded to have said at parting from him. "I hope you will soon be back with us. Remember this is your home. I begin to wish for rest. House, patients, carriage, all are here ready for you. Take your fancy out, and come back soon."

Leaving London, Sheridan Knowles began his career as a player in Bath, from whence he journeyed to Dublin. Here his uncle by marriage, the Rev. Peter Le Fanu, strove to combat his resolution of adopting the stage, by recommending other pursuits where his talents would find due recognition. But, being unable to dissuade him from his intentions, Mr. Le Fanu threw open his doors to Sheridan Knowles, who had frequent opportunities of exhibiting such dramatic powers as he possessed to fashionable gatherings assembled in the clergyman's drawing-rooms. He speedily made many friends in the Irish capital, especially amongst the collegians, who, impressed by his elocution, frequently accompanied him in numbers to Phœnix Park, that they might hear him deliver Shakespearian soliloquies.

He eventually made his *début* as Hamlet, at Crow Street Theatre, but his representation of the melancholy Prince being unsuccessful, no engagement followed. He therefore left Dublin, and joined Smithson's company, then playing in Wexford. Here he acted as a general utility man in the five-act tragedies and romantic dramas, which delighted audiences in the early part of this century. Alternately he was a lover in doublet and hose; a villain in cloak and vizard; and an *entr'acte* singer, whose vocal powers gained vast applause. His performance of a lover's part was not, however, confined to the creaking boards of Smithson's stage; for amongst the company were two young Scotch lasses, named Maria and Catherine Charteris, with the elder of whom he became enamoured. The fortunes of each were equally poor, but both were rich in hope, and the world lay all before them. Sheridan Knowles wooed; Maria Charteris was won; and they were married on the 29th of October, 1809.

Soon after their union they left Wexford and joined Cherry's company in Waterford, which numbered amongst its members young Edmund Kean, now in his twenty-first year. The great tragedian was then struggling with fate, and striving for fame. He had frequently played on

the same night the parts of King Richard III.
and Harlequin ; and on other occasions Douglas,
in Hannah More's tragedy of *Percy*, and The
Monkey in *La Perouse*. He had, moreover, as
Macbeth, counterfeited pangs of remorse whilst
suffering acute pains from hunger. Sharing his
friendship and admiring his abilities, Sheridan
Knowles conceived the idea of writing a play
for him, and accordingly produced a drama called
*Leo ; or, the Gipsy*, in which Kean represented
the hero. The piece, being received with great
favour, was considered by the chief actor so suitable to his capacities, that years after he was
anxious his first appearance before a London
audience should be made in the character of
Leo.   From Waterford, Knowles travelled to
Belfast, where, at the request of his new manager,
Mr. Montagu Talbot, he wrote another piece,
*Brian Boroihme*. Becoming a favourite with the
town, it was continually played during the season.
For this successful drama Mr. Montagu Talbot
paid him the sum of five pounds.

Feeling somewhat disgusted with his profits as
an author, and weary of his life as a player,

Knowles became anxious to secure other means by which he might earn an independent income for himself, his wife, and his new-born child. A certain clergyman named Groves, who had constantly attended the theatre, learning his desire, offered him the post of master to a public seminary. This he accepted with gratitude, and his salary, aided by fees for tuition, soon secured him a comfortable competence. He subsequently opened a school of his own, and here and in Glasgow, to which town he subsequently moved, he continued a teacher for many years. His love for dramatic composition survived the drudgery of his calling. Before leaving Belfast he had written a tragedy, *Caius Gracchus,* which had been produced in that city, and, according to the *News Letter*, received "the rapturous plaudits of a crowded house." He carried the play with him to Scotland, and waited a proper opportunity for its production. This seemed to present itself when Edmund Kean, making a tour of the provinces, visited Glasgow.

Since Sheridan Knowles had last seen him, Edmund Kean had made his appearance at Drury

R

Lane, and electrified London audiences by the brilliancy of his genius. He who had wanted bread, and consorted with inferiors, now possessed riches and was courted by the great. He who was unknown had become famous. Crowds applauded and critics praised him; he could experience poverty or dwell in obscurity no more. Full of delight and expectation, Sheridan Knowles, taking with him the manuscript of *Caius Gracchus*, hastened to greet and congratulate his old friend and fellow-player ; but Edmund Kean received him with a sense of the difference now marking their positions, and when the poor schoolmaster offered the successful actor his play, the latter loftily replied he had a dozen tragedies already awaiting his judgment. The mortified author replied none might be found equal to his ; when Kean made answer if *Caius Gracchus* was left it would receive due attention. Hurt by the manner of his reception, Knowles refused to accept this suggestion, and, putting the manuscript in his pocket, bade the player farewell.

The pain of disappointment was gradually overcome in the drudgery of school life ; visions of fame gradually vanished before the performance of commonplace duties. Another year passed, and once more the great Edmund Kean was announced to appear in Glasgow. Probably conscience had smitten him since his previous visit, for now he called on Sheridan Knowles, behaved with friendliness, and suggested he should write a play on the subject of Virginius, for the production of which at Drury Lane he promised to use his influence. Delighted at this proposal the schoolmaster's dreams of success returned to him, and he resolved on producing a great tragedy. Thirteen hours daily were spent in teaching, but such odd moments as he could spare were devoted to dramatic composition. If the Muses deigned to visit him whilst in the schoolroom, he rushed away to inscribe their inspirations on the first piece of paper which presented itself; and once, indeed, the poetic frenzy seizing him when he was engaged in explaining a problem in arithmetic, he wrote some lines on a slate, afterwards promoted to the dignity of a relic, and preserved with conscious pride by the playwright's admiring spouse.

At the end of three months *Virginius*, a
tragedy in five acts, being completed, Knowles
awaited the rewards of fame and fortune due
to his efforts. But, alas, fresh disappointment
attended him. On communicating with Edmund
Kean, the latter informed him a play on the
same subject, in which he was to represent the
part of Virginius, had already been accepted
at Drury Lane. This was a cause of bitter
vexation and sore distress to the poor schoolmaster. Fortune apparently frowned on his most
earnest endeavours. His keen depression, however, relaxed with time, and was presently van-
quished; for, taking heart of grace, the author
succeeded in having his tragedy produced in
the Glasgow Theatre. Though indifferently
played it met with considerable applause, and
was repeated for fourteen consecutive nights
before crowded audiences.

Amongst others who witnessed it was a certain
Mr. Tait, a friend of Macready; and Tait, being
impressed by the opportunities the character of
Virginius afforded, immediately wrote to the
great actor concerning *Virginius*. He described

the author, as Macready records in his Reminiscences, as a man of original genius, in whose
fortunes many of his fellow-citizens were interested. "It so happened," writes the actor,
"that I had undergone the reading of two or
three tragedies when late at Glasgow, and it
was with consequent distrust that, to oblige a
very good friend, I undertook to read this. Tait
was to send the manuscript without delay, and
I looked forward to my task with no very
good will. It was about three o'clock one day
that I was preparing to go out, when a parcel
arrived containing the letter from Tait and the
manuscript of *Virginius.* After some hesitation
I thought it best to get the business over, to do
at once what I had engaged to do, and I sat
down determinedly to my work. The freshness
and simplicity of the dialogue fixed my attention.
I read on and on, and was soon absorbed in
the interest of the story and the passion of
its scenes, till at its close I found myself in
such a state of excitement that for a time I
was undecided what step to take. Impulse
was in the ascendant, and snatching up my

pen I hurriedly wrote, as my agitated feelings prompted, a letter to the author, to me then a perfect stranger. I was closing my letter as the postman's bell was sounded up the street, when the thought occurred to me, what have I written? It may seem wild and extravagant; I had better reconsider it. I tore up the letter, and sallying out hastened directly to my friend Procter's lodgings, wishing to consult him and test by his the correctness of my own judgment. He was from home; and I left a card requesting him to breakfast with me the next day, having something very remarkable to show him. After dinner at a coffee-house I returned home, and in a more collected mood again read over the impassioned scenes, in which Knowles has given heart and life to the characters of the old Roman story. My first impressions were confirmed by a careful reperusal, and in sober certainty of its justness I wrote my opinion of the work to Knowles, pointing out some little oversights, and assuring him of my best exertions to procure its acceptance from the managers, and to obtain the highest payment for it. I have not preserved a copy of my letter, but its general purport may be guessed from the reply to it, which is here verbatim :

GLASGOW, 20*th April*, 1820.

MY DEAR SIR,

For bare sir is out of the question — I thank you from the bottom of my heart for the most kind, I must not say flattering, though most flattering, letter that you have written to me. Really I cannot reply to it in any manner that will satisfy myself, so I shall only once for all repeat, I thank you ! and feel as if I should never forget the opening of a correspondence with Mr. Macready. You must have a very warm heart. Do not think, I entreat you, that because I express myself imperfectly—very imperfectly—there is any deficiency where there ought not to be.

I 'have but a few minutes, I should say moments, to write. All your suggestions I have attended to ; I believe so, and if I have not I fully propose to attend to them, except so far as the word " squeak " is concerned ; that word I know not how to lose for want of a fit substitute—

the smallest possible sound.  Find out a term and make the alteration yourself; or if you cannot and still wish an alteration, do what you like. I don't care about it, I merely submit the matter to you.  Oh, I have forgotten the word "cheer." What shall I do also in the way of finding a substitute for that word?

I cannot stop to write another line.  I am very much your debtor, and truly

Your grateful, humble Servant,

J. S. KNOWLES."

This letter, eminently characteristic of its simple-hearted writer, pleased Macready greatly, and being enlisted in Knowles' interests, he urged the manager to accept *Virginius*.  In this regard he encountered no difficulty, and accordingly the characters were promptly cast, Macready, Charles Kemble, and Miss Foote sustaining the principal parts.  Macready's enthusiasm concerning the tragedy was unbounded; he read it to the company, and arranged the action and grouping of the crowds.  "My heart was in the work," he writes, "so much so that it would seem my zeal ran the risk of outstripping discretion, for it was made a complaint by Egerton that 'the youngest man in the theatre should take on him to order and direct his elders.' On Fawcett's report of this to me, I directly made the *amende* to Egerton, apologising for any want of deference I might have shown to my brother actors."

Day and night the images *Virginius* presented were before him, whilst "every vacant hour was employed in practice to give smoothness to those pathetic touches, and those whirlwinds of passion in the part, which in the full sway of their fury required the actor's self-command to ensure the correctness of every tone, gesture, and look."

Rehearsals had been carefully superintended, and final preparations made, when the manager was alarmed one morning on a demand being made by George IV. for sight of the manuscript, which had already passed the Lord Chamberlain's office. This being complied with, the royal decision was awaited with fear and trembling. However, the tragedy was returned next day, merely having some passages on tyranny erased, which his majesty feared would bear too personal a significance.

On the 17th of May, 1820, *Virginius* was produced for the first time. Great expectations concerning its merits were entertained by the town, and a crowded house gathered to witness the performance. And in the pit sat Sheridan Knowles, by turns radiant with hope and dejected by fear. The first act fell flat on an audience filled with high anticipations; even the second act failed to affect the house, principally because Charles Kemble, who suffered from a heavy cold, could scarce be heard; but, suddenly regaining his voice, in the third act he aroused interest and gained applause. Macready, inspired by enthusiasm, played with unusual fervour. In the character of Virginius, to quote the *Times* of the following morning, "he touched the passions with a more masterly hand, and evinced deeper pathos than on any former occasion." Interest now deepened to enthusiasm; cheers greeted the conclusion of every act; sobs and exclamations attended the great catastrophe where Virginius stabs his daughter, and the curtain fell on a house excited by terror and delight.

The tragedy took the town by storm. "Peals of approbation," says the *European Magazine*, "attended the announcement of this successful tragedy." It was played for fourteen nights, and revived next season with unabated interest. Knowles was advised to have it printed immediately, that he might reap remuneration from its sale. To aid him in this respect Macready called on his friend John Murray, and requested he would publish *Virginius*. Mr. Murray promised he would give it his consideration, but acting on the advice of his reader, the Rev. H. Milman, afterwards Dean of St. Paul's, he returned the manuscript in a few days with thanks. Knowles then offered it to Ridgway, of Piccadilly, who at once accepted it, and in the course of a couple of months it passed into several editions. It was dedicated to Macready in the form of a letter, running as follows:

" MY DEAR SIR,

" What can I do less than dedicate this

tragedy to you? This is a question which you cannot answer, but I can. I cannot do less; and if I could do more I ought and would.

"I was a perfect stranger to you; you read my play, and at once committed yourself respecting its merits. This perhaps is not saying much for your head, but it says a great deal for your heart; and that is the consideration which above all others makes me feel happy and proud in subscribing myself,

"Your grateful Friend and Servant,

"JAMES SHERIDAN KNOWLES."

Receiving the first copy of *Virginius* on a certain Saturday in May, the author resolved on personally presenting it to the dedicatee. No opportunity for the accomplishment of his desire presented itself on that or the following day, and as Knowles had arranged to leave town on Monday morning, he sought Macready on Sunday evening at the house of Sir Robert Kemeys in Park Lane, where the actor was dining. Before dinner ended, Macready was informed by a servant "a person" wanted to see him. "Utterly ignorant," writes the tragedian, "of any business that any one could have with me I was a good deal embarrassed; but Sir Robert very good-naturedly relieved me by saying, 'You had better see the person, Mr. Macready'; and accordingly I went into the hall, where to my astonishment in the dusk of the evening, I distinguished Knowles. 'How are you?' was his greeting. 'Good Heavens, Knowles, what is the matter? You should not have come here to me,' was my hasty remark. 'Oh, I beg your pardon,' he replied, 'I am going out of town in the morning, and I wished to give you this myself. Good-bye,' thrusting a parcel into my hand and hurrying away. Putting it into my pocket without looking at it, I returned in some confusion to the dinner-table. When I reached home I found the packet to contain the printed copy of *Virginius*, dedicated to myself, and a note sent after to my lodgings, expressive of his regret for intrusion on me, and evidently under wounded feelings, informing me it was the first copy struck off, and bidding me farewell. I wrote immediately to him explaining the awkwardness of my position, and my ignorance of his object in coming to me, and wishing to see him. The note reached him in the morning; he came at once, and all was made perfectly smooth between us."*

After many struggles James Sheridan Knowles had become a famous dramatist. Critics lauded him ; his old friend Charles Lamb congratulated him in verse ; the manager of Covent Garden Theatre paid him four hundred pounds. Elated with hope and encouraged by success he resolved to labour afresh, and set about rewriting his tragedy, *Caius Gracchus*, which was accepted and acted at Drury Lane for seven nights, a meed of success equalling its deserts. Two years later

---

* Many years later Macready presented the acting part of Virginius to Mr. John Forster, accompanying the gift with the following letter, preserved in the Dyce and Forster Libraries, South Kensington :

" I enclose the part of Virginius as delivered to me (after I read the play at Fawcett's request in his Covent Garden green-room, April 20th) from the Covent Garden copyist, poor old Hill. (You will see that even the skill of copying out parts is declined with our declining drama !) It has been in use with me above thirty years. You will smile at the Latin memoranda or suggestions to excite my feelings ! These I used to write in Latin, sometimes in Greek, sometimes in Italian, because as at that time I

and the schoolmaster, still toiling at Glasgow, had produced a five-act drama called *William Tell*, in which Macready played the hero. It was received with applause, and acted eleven consecutive nights. The author's next venture was a comedy called *The Blind Beggar of Bethnal Green;* the plot being taken from a ballad of that name. The selection was not happy, and the treatment but indifferent. The play was first tendered to the manager of Covent Garden, and "after long discussions and delays on the subject of value and price, rejected." It was then offered to and accepted by the Drury Lane management, and produced on the 28th of

could not command a dressing-room exclusively to myself, I did not choose that any one who might be 'chummed' with me should look over, or rather should understand my notes. No fear of any of them penetrating beyond English! I send you also the identical parchment I used on my first performance of this character, and which I have kept, with a sort of superstitious partiality till it has become what you see, ever since. It amazes yet pleases me these things have interest in your eyes—they have none in mine. A deep melancholy is on me in thinking and feeling that I shall never again excite the sympathies of those to whom I feel a sort of absolute affection."

November, 1828. Deficient in interest, false in construction, and incoherent in plot, its fate was speedily determined. The first act being dull, and the second promising no amendment, the audience, resenting its production, hissed, hooted, and sought to hinder its further progress. Therefore the stage manager came forward, and entreated "they would give the comedy a fair hearing, and not hastily and inconsiderately condemn it." He pledged his word the piece would not be repeated if, at its termination, their opinions of its merits continued unfavourable. It was then suffered to proceed, but not without frequent interruptions of hisses, cat-calls, and cries. The *Morning Chronicle* of the following day felt assured Knowles had enemies in the house, "who very early commenced their operations of condemnation." Of course, remarks that organ, "all the friends of Covent Garden would be desirous of opposing the comedy at Drury Lane, and that without the smallest interference on the part of the management of the rival theatre. We entirely acquit them of such practices—they are above it; but we cannot forget that at this moment Covent Garden is closed, and not a few of the underlings and retainers of that establishment, who would otherwise be occupied, are disengaged. This circumstance might, we only say might, contribute to procure Mr. Knowles a less equal tribunal."

The author, not being in town, was spared all pain of witnessing the reception of his comedy; when news of its fate reached it was powerless to depress him. "I remember as a child," writes his son, Richard Brinsley, "being with him in the Trongate on the day when the London papers came with intelligence that *The Beggar's Daughter* had come to grief, and Glasgow never saw him with a cheerier face, more hopeful, more assured. Friends tried to console him with the possibility that the comedy would be performed again and might rally. He knew better, and he kept the worst steadily before him, with unshaken confidence that success would come one day. Heaven had gifted him with the inestimable faculty of looking at the bright side of things, and in the midst of all his troubles, those ignoble pecuniary ones which seem to be

s

the plague and the nurse of genius, he took up his pen, determined not to be beaten."

To prove he could write a successful comedy now became the object of his life, and he immediately commenced the play by which his name is best remembered, *The Hunchback.* To follow the bent of his inclinations he for a while neglected a suggestion made by Macready, that he should write a drama having Alfred the Great for its hero. The new work was continued under disturbing circumstances. His pupils having diminished in number, possibly because failing to receive the attention formerly given them, Sheridan Knowles became a public lecturer; and, that he might exercise this calling with greater advantage, moved with his wife and family to Newhaven, close by Edinburgh. Here he laboured incessantly, teaching, writing, and lecturing. Macready, whilst fulfilling an engagement in the capital, called on him for the purpose of expostulating on his again attempting a form of dramatic composition in which he had previously failed. By way of meeting his objections Knowles read him the first act of *The Hunchback*, when the great player, ceasing all remonstrance, bade him continue his comedy. "This," says the author, "I thought the happiest of omens, for many a proof had he given me of his admirable judgment in such things."

He therefore worked with renewed spirit not only at *The Hunchback* but at *Alfred*, and in 1832 brought both plays to town. *Alfred* was produced on the 28th of that month, Macready playing the hero, and was pronounced a success. *The Hunchback* was also accepted ; but before the date fixed for its rehearsal arrived, Knowles showed the comedy to Morton, the dramatist, and to Macready, both of whom, with blended kindness and discrimination, pointed out the principal and secondary plots were independent of each other. Becoming convinced of this blemish, Knowles carried the comedy back to Newhaven and reconstructed the plot. In the course of some months it was again accepted at Drury Lane, and the author given to understand its rehearsal would commence immediately. In a few days, however, he received a letter from the management, stating it was found necessary to give another play prior representation, and the production of his comedy must therefore be postponed until next season.

Indignant at this treatment, Sheridan Knowles went to the theatre and demanded his manuscript. The manager expostulated, apologised, and finally offered to begin rehearsal at once ; but the enraged playwright insisted the play should be returned. When placed in his hands he took it to Covent Garden. This theatre, managed by Charles Kemble, had long been in difficulties, and was now on the verge of bankruptcy. Though acquainted with this fact, Sheridan Knowles offered Charles Kemble *The Hunchback*, which was immediately accepted. "And from that moment," says the author, "I found myself at home indeed, and among friends."

Miss Fanny Kemble, then in her twentieth year, records her first impressions of the comedy. "After my riding lesson," she writes, "I went and sat in the library to hear Sheridan Knowles' play of *The Hunchback*. Mr. Bartley and my father and mother were his only audience, and he read it himself to us. A real play, with real characters, individuals, human beings ; it is a good deal after the fashion of our old playwrights and does not disgrace its models. I was delighted with it; it is full of life and originality ; a little long, but that's a trifle. I like the woman's part exceedingly, but am afraid I shall find it very difficult to act."

Again she mentions reading the comedy, and liking it better than before. At this period an historical play—*Francis I.*—written by her, was about being produced, and she compares it to *The Hunchback* in favour of the latter. She was cast for Julia, her representation of which Knowles subsequently acknowledged far outstripped his most sanguine hopes. Helen was played by Miss Taylor, and Sir Thomas Clifford by Charles Kemble. Harassed by anxiety and worn by exertions, it had been the manager's original intention not to take part in the play, as we learn from his daughter's words, which afford a touching picture of his distress at the time. "Tried on my dresses for *The Hunchback*, they will be beautiful," she writes. "The rehearsal was over long before the carriage came for me ; so I went into my father's room, and

read the newspaper, while he and Mr. Bartley
discussed the cast of Knowles's play. It seems
my father will not act in it. I am sorry for that;
it is hardly fair to Knowles, for no one else can
do it. My poor father seemed too bewildered to
give any answer, or even heed, to anything, and
Mr. Bartley went away. My father continued to
walk up and down the room for nearly an hour,
without uttering a syllable, and at last flung
himself into a chair and leaned his head and
arms on the table. I was horribly frightened,
and turned as cold as stone, and for some
minutes could not muster up courage enough to
speak to him. At last I got up and went to him,
and, on my touching his arm, he started up, and
exclaimed: 'Good God, what will become of us
all?' I tried to comfort him, and spoke for a
long time, but much, I fear, as a blind man
speaks of colours. I don't know, and I don't
believe any one knows, the real state of terrible
involvement in which this miserable concern is
wrapped. What I dread most of all is that my
father's health will break down. To-day, while
he was talking to me, I saw him suddenly put

his hand to his side in a way that sent a pang through my heart. He feels utterly prostrated in spirit, and I fear he will work himself ill. God help us all. I came home with a heavy heart, and got ready my things for the theatre, and went over my part."

Charles Kemble eventually appeared in the comedy, as did likewise the author, who came to this resolution believing his appearance would create additional attraction. He therefore essayed the character of Master Walter. On the 5th of April, 1832, *The Hunchback* was produced for the first time. The crowded audience which assembled to witness the performance was unanimous in its appreciation. From the first act to the last hearty approbation was most liberally bestowed, and during the latter scenes between Julia, Clifford, and Master Walter, "the audience was overwhelmed with tears." When the curtain fell, the *Morning Chronicle* states : " The applause was tumultuous, and a general call being made for Knowles, Charles Kemble led him forward, obviously with no very good will, and as certainly with no very good grace. He was confused by

the novelty of his situation, and, whispering
Kemble, he said that, 'conscious as he was of
his own unworthiness, he presumed that the audience were applauding their own kindness.' This
Irishism was well received, and, after again
whispering Kemble, Knowles continued: 'Mr.
Kemble has desired me to say that the play
will be repeated on Saturday, and that Miss
Kemble's tragedy will be acted on Monday.'
Kemble audibly intimated his dissent from this
statement, and Knowles, shaking him heartily by
the hand, and in considerable agitation advancing
to the footlights, added with emphasis, 'Ladies
and gentlemen, allow my feelings of gratitude on
this occasion to triumph, and do not listen to
my friend Mr. Kemble. His daughter's tragedy
ought to be acted on Monday.' Much applause
and confusion followed, in the midst of which
Mr. Knowles retired, leaving Mr. Kemble in possession of the house (as they say elsewhere),
which he bespoke in these terms: 'It is but
common justice to Mr. Knowles to give out that
his play will be repeated every evening until
further notice.' The cheers, waving of hats,

handkerchiefs, and other demonstrations of satisfaction were as enthusiastic as they were general."

Meanwhile Sheridan Knowles, escaping from the glare and tumult which dazzled and confused him, ran panting to his dressing-room, and bolting the door, as he afterwards told a friend, "I sank down on my knees and from the bottom of my soul thanked God for His wondrous kindness to me. I was thinking on the bairns at home, and if ever I uttered the prayer of a grateful heart it was in that little chamber." The comedy ran to the close of the season, being only interrupted by three performances of *Francis I.*, some benefit nights, and the final appearances of Charles Young. It was played for the last time this season on the 22nd of June, an evening rendered eventful by the final performance of Charles Kemble and his daughter, who had made arrangements to visit America. When the curtain fell Bartley, coming forward, announced the farewell departure of the Kembles, and bespoke favour on behalf of the new management, when the audience called for Knowles and then clamoured for the Kembles, whom they rose to greet, waving hats and handkerchiefs enthusiastically. "It made my heart ache," writes Fanny Kemble, in whose simple words the scene is best described, "to leave my good, kind, indulgent audience—my friends, as I feel them to be; my countrymen, my English folk; my very worthy and approved good masters. And as I thought of the strangers for whom I am now to work in that distant, strange country to which we are going, the tears rushed into my eyes, and I hardly knew what I was doing. I scarcely think I even made my conventional curtsey of leave-taking to them, but I snatched my little nosegay of flowers from my sash and threw it into the pit with handfuls of kisses, as a farewell token of my affection and gratitude. And so my father, who was very much affected, led me off, while the house rang with the cheering of the audience. When we came off my courage gave way utterly, and I cried most bitterly. I saw numbers of people whom I knew standing behind the scenes to take leave of us." In this manner ended the last performance of *The Hunch-back* during its first season.

Sheridan Knowles, having made his reappearance on the stage in this comedy, continued an actor for many years. His efforts in this line of art were never marked by success. Nature had not gifted him with attributes necessary to a successful player. His stature was below the middle height, his person, now he had reached the age of eight-and-forty, was inclined to corpulency, and "his face, of rather fat intelligence," was inexpressive. The press pronounced him unsuited for the calling he had adopted, but Knowles, taking a different view, "was ravished with his own acting," as Macready records. However, in order to earn an independence for himself and his family, he was obliged either to play or teach, and he chose the former and less harassing labour. That his productions brought an inadequate income was due to the fact that before the Copyright Act passed managers were free to perform an author's plays without asking his permission or awarding him remuneration.

The tragedies and comedies Sheridan Knowles had written—*Virginius, Caius Gracchus, William Tell, Alfred the Great,* and *The Hunchback*—whose production occupied about twelve years, brought him but eleven hundred pounds, or not quite a hundred a year. Accordingly he became an actor, and played in the provinces and in America; not only representing the heroes of his own tragedies, but attempting such characters as Hamlet and Macbeth. He was apparently satisfied with his efforts. "To my brief success as an actor," he writes, "I owe what I should in vain have looked for as an author—emancipation from debt, a decently furnished house, the means of giving my children ample education, relief from the doubt whether to-morrow might not bring short commons, or none at all."

It is worth mentioning that James Sheridan Knowles in his last years became a Baptist minister. For in his day this man played many parts.

# LORD LYTTON'S PLAYS.

THE DUCHESS DE LA VALLIÈRE, first produced, 4th January, 1837.

THE LADY OF LYONS, first produced, 15th February, 1838.

RICHELIEU, first produced, 7th March, 1839.

THE SEA CAPTAIN, first produced, 16th July, 1839.

MONEY, first produced, 8th December, 1840.

NOT SO BAD AS WE SEEM, first produced, 14th May, 1851.

THE RIGHTFUL HEIR, first produced, 3rd October, 1868.

JUNIUS; OR, THE HOUSEHOLD GODS, first produced, 26th February, 1885.

Macready Meets Bulwer—The Actor Makes a Suggestion—*The Duchess de la Vallière*—First Representation—Unfavourable Reception — *The Lady of Lyons* — Curiosity of the Town — The Plot of an Historical Drama—Letters from the Playwright—*Richelieu* in the Greenroom—First Night of *Richelieu*—Criticism of the *Times*—*The Sea Captain*—Macready at the Haymarket —Production of *Money*—First-Night Demonstration—*Not so Bad as We Seem*—*Junius; or, The Household Gods.*

WHILST fulfilling an engagement in Dublin, in the month of October, 1834, Macready was introduced by Colonel D'Aguilar's to Mr. Edward Lytton Bulwer. The author, then in his thirty-first year, had acquired a literary reputation seldom gained by one so young. Possessing a vivid imagination, brilliant talents, and scholarly lore, he had by incessant hard work rendered his name familiar to the reading public. At the age of twenty-three he had written a romance entitled Falkland, which elicited considerable attention. Its success was indeed sufficient to procure him an offer of five hundred pounds for a second novel from Colburn, one of the most eminent London publishers. Accordingly Mr. Bulwer wrote Pelham. The manuscript was condemned by one of Colburn's readers and praised

by another.    Eventually the book being published, was received by the critics with abuse
and by the public with favour.    Mr. Bulwer
next produced The Disowned, a book praised
for "its lofty eloquence"; a phrase fitly describing
the author's style, but one scarce commending it
to modern taste.    Twelve months later was published Devereux, a work he ultimately found
"the least generally popular of his writings."    His
fame gradually widening, his name increased in
market value, so that for his third novel he received eight hundred pounds, and for his fourth
fifteen hundred.    Twelve months after Devereux's
appearance Paul Clifford was published; and
in 1831 he was returned Member of Parliament
for St. Ives, and appointed editor of the new
*Monthly Magazine.*

Next year Eugene Aram was before the
public, and in 1833 Godolphin, The Pilgrims
of the Rhine, and England and the English,
when the young author started for a holiday in
Italy.    His residence in that country suggested
the last days of Pompeii as a subject befitting romance, and with the restless energy and

ceaseless industry which characterised him, he wrote a novel, the scene of which was laid in the buried city. Returning to England he made arrangements for its publication, and then started out for Ireland. Whilst staying in Dublin, he encountered the famous Macready.

Still on the threshold of life, with his feet on the roadway of fame, Mr. Lytton Bulwer was sensible of the distinction he had gained in the past, and greatly hopeful of honours awaiting him in the future. The consciousness of merit, forced on him by public appreciation, probably accounted for the hauteur which largely marked his general bearing. "The simplicity of nature in thought, word, and deed was utterly foreign to his nature," writes his contemporary, Mr. S. C. Hall. Nor was Bulwer less proud of his distinguished talents than vain of his personal gifts, which, as the authority just quoted states, were enhanced by artificial aids. With delicate features, liquid eyes, and masses of dark hair, his appearance savoured of a melancholy Byronic hero; an unwholesome type not wholly passed from the surface of fashionable life in Mr. Bulwer's

T

early days.   Miss Harriet Martineau gives us an
etching of the young author as she, in 1832,
beheld him "seated on a sofa, sparkling and
languishing among a set of female votaries, he
and they dizened out, perfumed, and presenting
the nearest picture to a seraglio to be seen on
British ground."   Sensitive as became one who
intuitively perceives, variable as befitting the
temperament of an artist, he was brilliant and
morbid by turns, glad and sad in the self-same
hour, sanguine and depressed in a breath.

Macready, encountering him in a happy
moment, found him "very good-natured and, of
course, intelligent."   During their conversation
the actor urged him to write a play.   Mr.
Bulwer made answer he had already anticipated
this desire, but the greater portion of his attempt
was lost.   Before evening passed they had become sufficiently friendly to hope they might soon
meet in London.

Seven months later, at John Forster's pleasant
dinner-table, they again encountered.   Becoming
more intimate on this occasion, Macready a few
days later invited Bulwer to dine with him.

His courtesy was declined, in a letter which referred to " the honour of his acquaintance." This sentence grated on the actor's ear. " My acquaintance," he says, " can be no honour to such a man as Bulwer, and it almost seems like irony." Macready, foolishly ashamed of an art which afforded him distinction, and rendered him the desired associate of men and women celebrated for their talent or notable for their rank, under-estimated his social station, and continually apprehended slight and irony where neither was intended. A note in his diary aptly illustrates the extent of his weakness on this point. On attending the Literary Fund dinner, within eight days of the receipt of Bulwer's letter, he was informed his name was on the list of toasts. This disturbed him, as he felt unable to speak in public, from lack of habit and consciousness of uncertainty of his position. " I read in every newspaper of this week," he writes, " that my art is a very humble one—if indeed it be an art at all—and that its professors are entitled to little respect; and here, when in courtesy I am admitted as Mr. Macready among the esquires of the Royal Academy, the King's Printing Office, the *Quarterly Review*, etc. etc., I am to speak without the possibility of knowing what place is allowed me as an artist, or what degree of particular consideration may be extended to me as a man consistent in his private character."

A few months later, in February, 1836, Macready called on Bulwer, and found him in handsomely furnished chambers in the Albany. On repeating his suggestion made in Dublin to Bulwer that he should write a play, the author admitted he had since attempted a drama on the subject of Louise de la Vallière, but feared it was unworthy his visitor's powers, as the principal interest of the plot centred in a heroine. However, he felt anxious Macready should read the play, and give an opinion of its merits. The actor, having complied with this desire, again called on Bulwer, commended his work generally, mentioned certain objections, and suggested alterations which, after some protestations, the author consented to make.

They next proceeded to a question of terms. Bulwer demanded two hundred pounds down, and five pounds a night to be paid during the representation of his drama the two following seasons, after which the copyright should revert to him.

Before agreeing to this demand, Bunn, lessee of Drury Lane Theatre, where Macready was then engaged, was anxious to see the manuscript, that he might gauge the chances of its success. Bulwer was, however, unwilling to gratify his desire, as he considered it "precisely of that nature which no author of moderate reputation concedes to a publisher." A writer, he adds, "can have but little self-respect who does not imagine, in any new experiment in literature, that no risk can be greater than his own." Bunn continuing to consider himself justified in making the demand, and Bulwer in refusing compliance, the project of placing *The Duchess de la Vallière* on the stage of Drury Lane was, therefore, fortunately for its manager, abandoned.

At this point Mr. Morris, of the Haymarket Theatre, consented to grant the dramatist his terms; but, his company being indifferent performers, Bulwer wisely declined the offer. Finally, Macready having migrated to Covent Garden

Theatre, the manager of which, Mr. David Webster Osbaldiston, being willing to accept the drama, it was secured for that house. In November, the play was read in the manager's room to the company, who seemed greatly pleased with it; but, says Macready, recording the fact, " I cannot place much confidence in them." The *Athenæum* subsequently remarks it had seldom heard green-room report so loud in praise of any forth-coming drama, "which is only another proof," it adds, after the performance of the play, "of how very little that source of private information is to be relied on."

The first representation of *The Duchess de la Vallière* was fixed for Wednesday, the 4th of January, 1837, with the following cast : Marquis de Bragelonne, Macready; Louis XIV., H. Vandenhoff; Duke de Lauzun, W. Farren ; Marquis de Montes-pan, B. Webster; Mdlle. de la Vallière, Miss Helen Faucit. The play had been published on the previous day, and the *Morning Post* had devoted two columns to extracts from its most striking scenes; a form of advertisement which attracted general attention. Accordingly, on the evening of its first representation, a brilliant audience assembled in Covent Garden Theatre to witness the performance. But as the drama proceeded curiosity gave way to weariness, expectation was succeeded by disappointment. All Macready's great efforts were unable to save it from an impending fate of damnation.

"A most numerous, and certainly the most patient audience we ever recollect to have sat amongst," says the *Times* of the following day, "last night witnessed the first performance of Mr. E. L. Bulwer's long-promised play of *The Duchess de la Vallière*, the success of which, considering the vast number of the author's personal friends present on the occasion, was equivocal." Through five long acts, vapid bathos, false sentiments, strained similes, inflated sentences, surface philosophies were unsparingly inflicted on suffering hearers. "It has never been our lot," says the *Times*, "to witness a more favourable and indulgent audience. Whenever there was an opportunity for applauding it was seized with zeal, and the house rang again with acclamations. This was the case once or twice in the first and second acts, and again in the fourth and fifth; but all these vehement and well-intentioned efforts to save the author and themselves, would not do; the drowsy influence prevailed, and at one time we almost expected to see the whole house fast asleep. The curtain, however, did not fall to relieve them until a quarter past eleven, when a strong contest took place between the contents and the non-contents. This was put an end to by a call for Mr. Macready and Miss Faucit, which was quickly attended to. The lady and gentleman having gone through the formula made and provided on such occasions, retired. Mr. Pritchard then came forward to give out the play, but the noise occasioned by one set of wags who called for Bulwer, and of another who bawled for Vandenhoff,* prevented us from ascertaining whether the play was given out or not. When Mr. Pritchard quitted the stage, the house had in a great degree subsided, and we left the theatre not supposing that Mr. Bulwer would gratify his admirers by exhibiting himself."

Concerning *The Duchess de la Vallière* the

---

* Who had performed his part in an execrable manner.

press was poor in praise. The *Morning Herald* thought its incidents weak, disconnected, and productive of no general effect. To the *Times* it appeared "a very dull and a very foolish play. No man, we think," says that organ, "but one whose vanity has been flattered most extravagantly within the circle of his own little coterie, no man who felt a due respect for the rules even of that *bienséance* by which society is generally governed, would have ventured to produce a drama, the subject of which is the heartless debaucheries of a profligate monarch, and his equally profligate courtiers. It is in the worst taste of the worst school, the school of modern French romance. As to the general style of the drama, as regards its diction it is neat and correct in the level parts, and emphatic and almost eloquent in two or three of the more serious scenes, but its general character is feebleness. There is much pettiness of expression, a plentiful harvest of words, but not many signs of sound or deep thinking. It is evident that Mr. Bulwer possesses but little skill in the art or craft of constructing plays."

In order to save its life if possible, the knife was liberally applied, and on a third representation it appeared much strengthened, but the drama was played to a half-empty house. "The claquers of the first night were absent," says the *Times*, "and the applause except in three instances was miserably feeble." It ran for four consecutive nights, and was played eight times in all during the month, after which *The Duchess de la Vallière* was withdrawn.

Failure but incited Mr. Bulwer towards fresh efforts. He determined to obtain success as a dramatist, equal to that he had already achieved as a novelist. Vain were the hopes of *Fraser's Magazine*, which trusted its remarks "would convince Mr. Bulwer the public were quite right in practically dissuading him from a path he is evidently not born to tread with gratification to others or advantage to himself." Before many months had passed, he had begun a new play called *The Adventurer*, a title subsequently altered, at Macready's suggestion, to *The Lady of Lyons*. The chief incidents of its plot had been suggested by a tale named The Bellows Menders, and the drama was undertaken chiefly out of sympathy with Macready's new enterprise as manager of Covent Garden Theatre. Believing the critics had dealt hardly by *The Duchess de la Vallière*, through prejudices they entertained towards its writer, he resolved the new drama should be produced anonymously. Therefore to Macready alone was the secret of its authorship confided.

*The Lady of Lyons* was in rehearsal in the early part of 1838, and on the evening of Thursday, the 15th of February, was announced for representation. The following is the original cast: Beauséant, Elton; Glavis, Meadows; Colonel Damas, Bartley; Deschappelles, Strickland; Landlord, Yarnold; Gaspar, Diddear; Claude Melnotte, Macready; Officers, Howe, Pritchard, and Roberts; Madame Deschappelles, Miss Clifford; Pauline, Miss Helen Faucit; Widow Melnotte, Mrs. Griffith; Janet, Mrs. East; Marian, Miss Garrick.

Curiosity had for some time been excited by rumours regarding the power and brilliancy of this play; the first representation was therefore attended by an unusually large audience. Men and women of rank and fashion filled the

boxes, the pit and galleries swarmed to over-
flowing. The curtain ascended, and the drama
began amidst breathless excitement. Macready
had never played with greater force and energy.
Miss Faucit acted with grace and dignity; before
the first act concluded it was argued the drama
would prove successful. Curiosity regarding the
author was now rife; a thousand surmises were
made as to his name. None seemed to recognise
it as Bulwer's production. Mr. and Mrs. S. C.
Hall remembered John Forster coming into their
box, and on Bulwer's name being mentioned as
the playwright, protesting in good faith against
the assumption, feeling sure if Bulwer had written
the play he would have confided the secret to
him.

As the drama proceeded applause increased.
Miss Faucit betrayed an *abandon* that not merely
won plaudits but drew tears from the audience.
" Her first indication of changed feeling," says
the *Morning Chronicle*, " from agony to rage,
at the word mother addressed to the widow
Melnotte, was an exquisite touch of genuine
nature." The while Bulwer was not present to

witness the triumph of his production, being
detained in the House of Commons by a debate
on the ballot in which he took part. Seizing the
earliest moment duty permitted him, he hastened
from St. Stephen's. Before quitting its precincts
he encountered a member just returned from
Covent Garden Theatre. With many hopes and
fears struggling in his breast, Bulwer questioned
him on the success of the new drama. ' The other
replied indifferently ; " H'm, it's very well for that
sort of thing." Still in suspense, he hurried towards the playhouse and entered Lady Blessington's box. The curtain had risen on the last act :
the audience followed the players' movements
with rapt attention, hearkened to their words
with thirsty ears, and finally, as the curtain fell,
burst into a loud tumult of prolonged applause.
Lady Blessington looked towards Bulwer question-
ingly. " It's very well for that sort of thing," he
said, as he hurried away to Westminster for the
division.

Though the public was loud in its approbation
of the new drama, the press was not blind to its
demerits. " It was most industriously applauded,

throughout, though not without an occasional dash of sibillation," says the *Morning Post*, " but at the close the applause was furious. Some striking situations, some direct appeals to the most eminent sources of strong feeling in the human breast; but above all the very excellent acting of Miss Helen Faucit saved this foolish play from the condemnation which many better plays have received. The author, whose name we learn is Calvert, was doubtless made very happy by the applause of the audience, and we offer him our congratulations. But we think his play is grievously wanting in one important quality—common sense. He makes his peasant talk sad stuff, such as a manly peasant would never talk, about his natural equality, and so on, with persons of family, just as if anybody, peasant or peer, with a grain of sense would ever doubt that. The peasant (we are vexed to see Macready playing so foolish a character) thinks that all true glory is to be sought for in the future, not in the past, and therefore that ancestry signifies nothing, also that a laurel is not a whit better that it has 'grown upon some forgotten grave.' The author seems to mistake extravagance for energy, and the stringing of pretty words together without sense or logical coherence for poetry. Pauline is the only one of the *dramatis personæ* to whom the author of the play accords permission to appear throughout something like a rational creature."

The *Times*, whilst admitting *The Lady of Lyons* possessed "the merit of artificial construction," and contained "several nice speeches," declared the characters were "the gaudy overdrawn personages of melodrama." The *Morning Chronicle* was more favourably disposed towards the drama. "The play," says this journal, "which is said to be from the pen of Mr. Chorley, is remarkably well constructed. Not a scene flags, the comic portions of the dialogues are full of pleasantries, and whenever impassioned it becomes poetical. The author has fairly grappled with the subject. He has dealt with love as dignified emotion, not indebted for its triumph over the pride of station to the freaks of accident, but to the energy of its own inspiration."

*The Lady of Lyons* was repeated nightly until the 23rd of February, when it was an-

nounced to be played every Tuesday, Thursday'
and Saturday until further notice.    Meanwhile
a section of the public were inclined to resent
certain expressions considered republican in principle contained in Claude Melnotte's flowery
speeches.    And this feeling gradually increasing, and promising to mar the popularity of the
drama, Macready thought it necessary on the
author's behalf and on his own, to disclaim,
in a speech delivered from the stage, all intentions of introducing politics in the play.

For nine days the dramatist's name was not
divulged.    Bulwer wanted to feel thoroughly
assured of his success before declaring himself
author of *The Lady of Lyons.*    As the play
continued to draw crowded houses, and the certainty of its fate was undoubted, he permitted
Macready to disclose their secret whenever he
pleased.    The latter therefore had the following
paragraph inserted under the advertisement of
his performance on the 24th of February :

" In announcing the name of Edward Lytton
Bulwer, Esq., as the author of *The Lady of Lyons,*
the manager cannot withhold the expression of

his grateful acknowledgment to that gentleman for the kind and liberal manner in which he has desired to testify his interest in the success of this theatre by the presentation of this drama."

In so much as the *Morning Post* had been deliberately led into error regarding the authorship of the drama, by receiving some passages from its scenes marked as "extracts from Mr. Calvert's new play," that organ now became indignant at the deception practised. Knowledge of the author, it contended, would not have changed its opinion of his play. "We find it difficult to believe," says that journal, "that a gentleman of any sort of literary eminence should have written it. We own it is our misfortune not to admire any of Mr. Bulwer's literary works; but we thought him above writing such a play as *The Lady of Lyons.* A thing so puerile in plot, so sickly in sentiment, so affected in phraseology, could not, we supposed, have been written by any one who had received a regular literary education."

Her Majesty, accompanied by her mother, the Duchess of Kent, and attended by the

U

Countess of Charlemont, Lady Carrington, and the Earl of Fingal, visited Covent Garden on the 6th of March to witness *The Lady of Lyons.* The Queen, being much gratified by the play, sent a message of congratulation to its author, and requested he would inform Macready how delighted she had been with his acting. Months later, Her Majesty again visited the theatre to see the same piece. When the curtain fell, Macready retired to his room and had undressed, when an equerry came with a message from the Queen desiring he would come on the stage as the audience were calling for him. He immediately dressed again, but not before receiving a second despatch from Her Majesty, on which he hurried before the footlights, and was received by enthusiastic applause in which she heartily joined. Returning to his room he donned a court suit, and waited in the ante-room through which the Queen presently passed. Lord Conyngham, who was in attendance, summoned him to her, when she said: "I have been very much pleased." At this he bowed profoundly, and lighted Her Majesty to her carriage.

On publishing *The Lady of Lyons*, Bulwer declared in a preface he had no intention of writing again for the stage, and therefore, so far as his own experiment was concerned he had but little to hope or fear. This resolution was, however, soon abandoned, and before many months elapsed he had conceived the idea of writing an historical drama. In the Dyce and Forster Libraries, a letter is preserved in which he narrates this project to Macready. The communication is of singular interest, as showing the difference between the original plot, and the play in its finished condition. It is dated September, 1838, and runs as follows:

"MY DEAR MACREADY,

"I have thought of a subject. The story full of incident and interest. It is to this effect. In the time of Louis XIII. The Chevalier de Marillac is the wittiest and bravest gentleman, celebrated for his extravagant valour and his enthusiasm for enjoyment; but in his most mirthful moments a dark cloud comes over him at one name—the name of Richelieu. He confides to his friend Cinq

U 2

Mars the reason, viz., he had once entered into a conspiracy against Richelieu : Richelieu discovered and sent for him. 'Chevalier de Marillac,' said he, 'I do not desire to shed your blood on the scaffold, but you must die. Here is a command on the frontier; fall in battle.' He went to the post, but met glory, and not death. Richelieu, reviewing the troops, found him still living, and said, 'Remember, the sword is over your head. I take your parole to appear before me once a quarter. You can still find death. I will give you time for it.' Hence his extravagant valour; hence his desire to make the most of life. While making this confidence to Cinq Mars, he is sent for by Richelieu. He goes as to death. Richelieu receives him sternly, reminds him of his long delay, upbraids him for his profligate life, etc. Marillac answers with mingled wit and nobleness; and at last, instead of sentencing him to death, Richelieu tells him that he has qualities that make him wish to attach him to himself, and that he will marry him to a girl with a great dowry, and give him high office at court. He must marry directly. Marillac goes out enchanted.

"Now, Richelieu's motive is this: Louis XIII. has fallen in love with this girl, Louise de la Porte, and wishes to make her his mistress. All the King's mistresses have hitherto opposed Richelieu. He is resolved that the King shall have no more. He will have no rival with the King. He therefore resolves to marry her to Marillac, whose life is in his power, whom he can hold in command, whom he believes to be too noble to suffer the adulterous connection.

"Marillac is then introduced, just married, with high appointments and large dowry, the girl beautiful, when, on his wedding-day, Cinq Mars tells him that the King loves his wife. His rage and despair—conceives himself duped. Scene with the girl, in which he recoils from her. Suddenly three knocks at the door. He is sent for by the King, and despatched to a distance; the bride, not wived, is summoned to court.

"Marillac, all pride and wrath, and casting all upon Richelieu, agrees to conspire against the Cardinal's life. The fortress where Richelieu lodges is garrisoned with the friends of the conspirators. Just as he has agreed, he received

an anonymous letter telling him that his wife is
at Chantilly; that she will sleep in the chamber
of the Montmorencies; that Louis means to enter
the room that night; that if he wishes to guard
his honour, he can enter the palace by a secret
passage which opens in a picture of Hugo de
Montmorenci, the last duke, who had been beheaded by Louis (an act for which the King
always felt remorse). This Montmorenci had
been the most intimate friend of Marillac, and
had left him his armour as a present. A thought
strikes Marillac, and he goes off the stage.

"Louise alone in this vast room—the picture
of Montmorenci in complete armour—a bed at the
end. She complains of her husband's want of
love, and laments her hard fate—dismisses her
women. The King enters and locks the doors;
after supplication and resistance on her part, he
advances to seize her, when from Montmorenci's
picture comes a cry of 'Hold!' and the form
descends from the panel and interposes. The
King, horror-stricken and superstitious, flies;
Louise faints. The form is Marillac. While she
is still insensible, the clock strikes; it is the hour

he is to meet the conspirators. He summons her women, and leaves her.

" Richelieu alone at night when Marillac enters to him, tells him his life is in his power, upbraids him for his disgrace, etc. Richelieu informs him that he has married him to Louise to prevent her dishonour, that he had sent the anonymous letter, etc., and converts Marillac into gratitude. But what is to be done ? The conspirators have filled the fortress. They (Richelieu and Marillac) retire into another room, and presently the conspirators enter the one they have left, and Marillac joins them and tells them the Cardinal is dead, that he will see to the funeral, etc., and they had better go at once and announce it to the King, and that there are no marks of violence, that it seems like a fit (being suffocation).

" SCENE IN THE STREETS OF PARIS.

" The King, who had always feared and hated Richelieu, hears the news, and is at first rejoiced, the courtiers delighted, Paris in a jubilee. But suddenly comes news of commotion, riot ; messengers announce the defeat of the armies ; the

Spaniards have crossed the frontiers, his general, de Feuguieres, is slain, hubbub and uproar without, with cries of 'Hurrah! the old Cardinal is dead,' etc., when there is a counter cry of 'The Cardinal, the Cardinal!' and a band of soldiers appear, followed by Richelieu himself in complete armour. At this sight the confusion, the amaze, etc., the mob changes humours, and there is a cry of 'Long live the great Cardinal!'

"SCENE, THE KING'S CHAMBER.

"The King, enraged at the trick played on him, and at his having committed himself to joy at the Cardinal's death, hears that De Marillac had announced the false report, orders him to the Bastille, tells the Count de Charost to forbid Richelieu the Louvre, and declares henceforth he will reign alone. Joy of the anti-Cardinalists, when the great doors are thrown open, and Richelieu, pale, suffering, sick, in his Cardinal's ' robes, leaning on his pages, enters and calls on Charost (the very man who is to forbid his entrance) to give him his arm, which Charost tremblingly does before the eyes of the King.

Richelieu and the King alone. Richelieu says he has come to tender his resignation, the King accepts it, and Richelieu summons six secretaries groaning beneath sacks of public papers, all demanding immediate attention. Richelieu retires to a distance, and appears almost dying. The King desperately betakes himself to the papers, his perplexity, bewilderment, and horror at the dangers round him. At last he summons the Cardinal to his side and implores him to resume the office. The Cardinal, with great seeming reluctance, says he only will on one condition, complete power over foes and friends; Louis must never again interfere with public business. He then makes him sign various papers, and when all is done the old man throws off the dying state, rises with lion-like energy: 'France is again France—to the frontiers. *I* lead the armies,' etc. (a splendid burst). Louis, half enfeebled, half ashamed, retires. Richelieu, alone, gives various papers to the secretaries, and summons Marillac and his wife. He asks her if she has been happy, she says, 'No,' thinking her husband hates her; puts the same question to Marillac, who, thinking she wishes to be separated, says the same. He then tells them as the marriage has not been fulfilled they can be divorced. They wofully agree, when turning to Marillac he shows him the King's order that he should go to the Bastille, and then adds that in favour of his service in saving his (Richelieu's) life, he has the power to soften his sentence, but he must lose his offices at court and go into exile. On hearing this Louise turns round, her love breaks out—she will go with him into banishment, and the reconciliation is complete. Richelieu, regarding them, then adds: 'Your sentence remains the same—we banish you still—Ambassador to Austria.'"

With this sketch he enclosed the following note, betraying the difficulties he foresaw and the diffidence he felt: "Now look well at this story, you will see that incident and position are good. But then there is one great objection. Who is to do Richelieu? Marillac has the principal part and requires you; but a bad Richelieu would spoil all. On the other hand if you took Richelieu, there would be two acts without you, which will never do; and the main interest of the plot

would not fall on you. Tell me what you propose. Must we give up this idea? The incidents
are all historical. Don't let me begin the thing
if you don't think it will do, and decide about
Marillac and Richelieu. Send me back the
papers. You can consult Forster of course."

Macready having made certain suggestions
obviating the difficulties mentioned, the drama
was proceeded with, and in November, 1838, the
manuscript was sent to the manager. In the
note accompanying it, Bulwer wrote: "Acts one
and three may require a little shortening, but
you are a master at that. The rest average the
length of the acts in *The Lady of Lyons.* I hope
the story is clear. The domestic interest is not
so strong as in *The Lady*, but I think the acting
of Richelieu's part may counterbalance this defect. For the rest I say of this as of *The Lady*,
if at all hazardous or uncertain it must not be
acted, and I must try again."

Determined to conquer he was willing to
labour; and wisely submitted his opinion as an
author to the judgment of Macready as an actor.

Again he writes to the manager : "I begin to despair of the play and of myself. Unless, therefore, upon consideration you see clearly what at present seems doubtful, the triumphant effect of the portraiture and action of Richelieu himself, you had better return me the play; and if I can form myself in a new school of art, and unlearn all that tact and thought have hitherto taught me, I will attempt another. But for this year you must do without me."

On reading the sketch submitted to him, Macready considered that though excellent in parts it was "deficient in the important point of continuity of interest;" and feared "the play would not do—or could not be made effective." He then read it to his wife and sister, and next day calling on Bulwer, made several suggestions for important alterations. At first the successful author combated the actor's judgments, but presently perceiving their justness, agreed to profit by their conclusions. "When I developed the object of the whole plan of alterations," writes Macready, "he was in ecstasies. I never saw him so excited, several times exclaiming he was 'enchanted' with the plan, and observed in high spirits, 'what a fellow you are.' He was indeed delighted. He is a wonderful man."

Next day, Bulwer brought him two scenes, and they settled the plot of the remainder. But yet Macready was dissatisfied. With delicate consideration for the author's susceptibilities, he wrote expressing to him how foremost in consideration was his reputation; "that his play would have been valuable from any other person, but that it would not serve his interest, whether in reference to his literary fame, his station, or his political position." In answer to this, Bulwer said: "I fully appreciate the manly and generous friendship you express so well, and have only one way to answer it. I had intended to turn to some other work already before me. But I will now lay all by, and neither think of, nor labour at anything else, until something or other be done to realise our common object. Send me back *Richelieu*; and if you think it possible, either by alterations or by throwing the latter acts overboard altogether, to produce such situations as may be triumphant, we will try again. The historical character of Richelieu is not to be replaced, and is therefore worth preserving. But if neither of us can think of such situations, we must lay his eminence on the shelf and try something else." Several suggestions of amendment were then made by Bulwer in a letter published some years since by the present Lord Lytton, in a paper entitled " The Stage in Relation to Literature," published in the *Fortnightly Review*.

The drama was rewritten once more, and again submitted to the manager, who found it "greatly improved, but still not quite to the point of success." In order to have the judgments of others on its merits, Macready invited a party of friends, amongst whom were Browning, Blanchard, Fox, Bintol, and Wallace, to hear it read the following Sunday, December 16th, 1838. On assembling, Macready requested they would not speak during the reading, but supplying them with pencils and paper, desired they might write their criticisms. Therefore they listened in silence ; and at the conclusion returned favourable opinions of the play. Macready immediately communicated these to the author, who replied by offering his thanks and expressing his misgivings. "The result is encouraging," he writes, "but at the risk of seeming over fearful, I must add also that it is not decisive. . . . Browning's short line of 'the play's the thing' is a laconism that may mean much or little. Besides he wants experience. Were I myself certain of the dramatic strength of the play (as I was in the case of *The Lady of Lyons*), I would at once decide on the experiment from the opinions you have collected. But I own I am doubtful, though hopeful, of the degree of dramatic strength in it ; and I remain just as irresolute now as I was before. I fancy that the effect on the stage of particular scenes cannot be conveyed by reading. Thus in the fifth act the grouping of all the characters round Richelieu, the effect of his sudden recovery, etc. No reading, I think, can accurately gauge the probable effect of this. And in the fourth act the clinging of Julie to Richelieu, the protection he gives her, etc., will have, I imagine, the physical effect of making the audience forget whether he is her father or not. There they are before you, flesh and blood, the old man and the young bride involved in the same fate, and creating the sympathy of a domestic relation. More than all my dependence on the stage, is my reliance on the acting of Richelieu himself, the embodiment of the portraiture, the look, the gesture, the personation, which reading cannot give. But still I may certainly overrate all this. For if the play do fail in interest, the character may reward the actor, but not suffice to carry off the play, especially as he is not always on the stage. On the whole, therefore, I am unable to give a casting vote; and I leave it to you with this assurance, that if it be withdrawn you shall have another play by the end of February."

He then agreed to a suggested test by which its fate should be determined. "Do you recollect," he asks Macready, "that passage in The Confessions, when Rousseau, haunted by vague fear that he was destined to be damned, resolved to convince himself one way or the other; and taking up a stone shied it at a tree?

If the stone hit, he was to be saved ; if it missed, he was to be damned. Luckily it hit the tree, and Rousseau walked away with his mind perfectly at ease. Let us follow this notable example. Our tree shall be in the greenroom. You shall shy at the actors. If it hit the mark well and good. If not we shall know our fate. To speak literally, I accept your proposal to abide by the issue of a reading to the actors ; though I remember that jury anticipated great things from *La Vallière,* and I think they generally judge according as they like their parts. The general tone of your friendly and generous letter induces me, indeed, to release you at once from the responsibility of the decision, and to say boldly that I am prepared to have the play acted. It can therefore be read with that impression to the greenroom, and if it does not take there, why it will not be too late to retreat. If it does, I can only say *make ready!* Present! Fire! All I could doubt was the theatrical interest of the story. Your account reassured me on that point, and there-

x

fore you will have fair play for your own art and genius in the predominant character."

On the 5th January, 1839, Macready read *Richelieu* to his company, and was "agreeably surprised to find it excite them in a very extraordinary manner. The expression of delight," he adds, "was universal and enthusiastic." During the whole of February and the early part of March the drama was in rehearsal at Covent Garden. Macready's labours to render it successful were incessant; but perhaps his greatest trouble arose in striving to grasp the Cardinal's character as depicted in the play. "Gave my attention," he writes in his diary, February 20th, "to the consideration of the character of Richelieu, which Bulwer has made particularly difficult by its inconsistency : he has made him resort to low jest, which outrages one's notions of the ideal of Cardinal Richelieu with all his vanity and subtleness and craft." Having read an account of the great statesman by D'Israeli, and heard the Comte de Vigny narrate several anecdotes illustrative of the character of Louis XIII., Richelieu, and Cinq Mars, the manager was yet more puzzled by the character he was to represent. Learning this, Bulwer sent him a list of books dealing with the Cardinal, but warned him none of them would afford much insight into the minister's manner; for the portrayal of which he would have to draw on his own genius. However, Bulwer conveys his idea of the character in one important point: "I know not if you conceive Richelieu's illness (Act V.) as I do?" he writes. "I do not mean it for a show illness. He is really ill, though he may exaggerate a little. When they are going to tear France from him, they do really tug at his heart-strings. He is really near fainting at the prospect of his experiment with the secretaries: and it is the mind invigorating the body, it is the might of France passing into him, which effects the cure. If there be delusion, it is all sublimed and exalted by the high-hearted truth at the bottom of it."

Nor was Macready's care confined to the representation of the Cardinal alone: as a great artist and careful manager he was anxious for the success of every member of his company. More especially was he desirous Mauprat and

Louis XIII. should be well represented, and accordingly he repeatedly read the parts of these characters with Anderson and Elton, the players to whom they were respectively entrusted. To the latter he interpreted various extracts from Anquetel and Cinq Mars, that he might illustrate the weakness of Louis' nature; when Elton went away feeling more at ease with his task.

For some time the manager found it difficult to obtain a fitting representation for François. "There are many allusions," wrote Bulwer, "to the youth of François, and the interest of the character so much depends upon his being young, that I have great doubts of the audience being sufficiently conscious of the great youth of Elton, wig him as you will." After some consideration, Macready concluded the part would best be represented by a woman, and accordingly offered it to Mrs. Warner. As, however, he had some years previously recommended her never to don male costume, she refused to depart from his advice. "I did not press the point," writes Macready, "for I expected her grounds of objection." The character was allotted to Mr. Henry Howe, then

in his twenty-sixth year, who played with satisfaction to his manager and the public. The
following is the original cast:

| | |
|---|---|
| Louis XIII. . . . . . | MR. ELTON. |
| Gaston, Duke of Orleans* . | . MR. DIDDEAR. |
| Baradas . . . . | . MR. WARDE. |
| Cardinal Richelieu . . | . MR. MACREADY. |
| Chevalier de Mauprat . . | . MR. ANDERSON. |
| Sieur de Beringhen . . | . MR. VINING. |
| Joseph, a Capuchin . . | . MR. PHELPS. |
| Huguet, an Officer . . | . MR. GEORGE BENNETT. |
| François, a Page . . . | . MR. HENRY HOWE. |
| First Courtier . . . | . MR. ROBERTS. |
| Captain of the Archers . | . MR. MATTHEWS. |
| First ⎫ | ⎧ MR. TILBURY. |
| Second ⎬ Secretaries of State . ⎨ | MR. YARNOLD. |
| Third ⎭ | ⎩ MR. PAYNE. |
| Governor of the Bastille . | . MR. WALDRON. |
| Gaoler . . . . | . MR. AYLIFFE. |
| Julie de Mortemar . . | . MISS HELEN FAUCIT. |
| Marion de Lorme . . | . MISS CHARLES. |

After months of patient toil and trouble
endured by actors and manager, *Richelieu* was
produced on the 7th of March, 1839. The morning
of that day, Macready lay in bed thinking over

---

* In the character of Gaston, Duke of Orleans, Mr.
Henry Irving made his first appearance on the stage, at
the Lyceum Theatre, Sunderland.

his part, then rising went to Covent Garden
and rehearsed the play, after which, tired and
anxious, he awaited the result of his endeavours.
Long before the curtain rose the house was
crowded to excess, a feeling of suppressed excitement pervaded the audience, expectation glowed
on every face. Presently, when in the second
act Richelieu was found seated in his study,
a storm of applause greeted Macready, who it
was noticed suffered from nervousness. Miss
Faucit's entrance was a signal for acclamation, and
throughout her acting was received with enthusiastic appreciation. The manager records losing
his self-possession on this night, and was obliged to
use too much effort. He, like all true artists, felt
dissatisfied with his endeavours, but how, he asks,
"Can a person get up such a play and do justice
at the same time to such a character?" His
exertions were, however, greeted with approval,
he possessed the sympathies of the house. The
drama likewise steadily gained in favour, and
when the curtain fell, says the *Times*, "Sir Lytton
Bulwer, according to the new and most absurd
fashion, being called for, made his bow from the

stage-box to a crowded audience." The *Morning Post* adds, the house cheered "with quite as much absurdity as enthusiasm, to get the author upon the stage. All this was the nonsense of popularity," continued that paper, "but the sense of it consisted in the triumph of the play."

The criticisms of *Richelieu* published next morning were not so flattering to Sir Lytton Bulwer, as the plaudits of those who had witnessed his play. The journal last quoted, whilst acknowledging it to be a work of talent, as regards plot, scene, and incident, declares the author is not a master of versification. "In short," it continues, "he is not a poet, and although this play is evidently his *chef-d'œuvre* in dramatic effort, if not indeed his crowning laurel in regard to his literary fame, as it now stands, yet it is very deficient in deep, fine, beautiful embodyings of true and eloquent thoughts and images which constitute poetry expressed in language equally eloquent and true. So far then it will not rank with our dramatic literature of the first class; but in other respects it is an ambitious and successful effort, and gives fair food for very high commendation." The *Times*, while pronouncing *Richelieu* clever, continues : " It reveals no great secrets of human nature; the general embellishments of the language are such as we had rather seen them omitted than retained.    But as exhibiting a knowledge of stage effect, the art of keeping alive the interest of an audience, the knack of bringing in a startling situation in the right place just where it was wanted, of dropping the act curtain at the proper time, as exhibiting all this the play has certainly the merit of a stirring, bustling, effective drama, with a very strong plot of affinity to the melodrama."

Seven months after the production of *Richelieu*, Sir Lytton Bulwer had a five-act drama, entitled *The Sea Captain*, in rehearsal.  This play had been submitted to the judgment of Macready, who had made various alterations in the manuscript and offered certain suggestions to the author.  During its rehearsal both Macready and Bulwer were anxious regarding its success and fearful of its fate.  On the 16th of July in this year (1839) Macready ended his connection with

Covent Garden Theatre, and on the 19th of August began his engagement under Webster at the Haymarket. At this theatre on the 31st of October, *The Sea Captain* was first produced with the following cast : Lord Ashdale, Mr. J. Webster; Sir Maurice Beevor, Mr. Strickland; Norman, Mr. Macready; Falkner, Mr. Howe; Onslow, Mr. Phelps; Gausseu, Mr. O. Smith; Luke, Mr. Gallott; Lady Arundel, Mrs. Warner; Violet, Miss Helen Faucit; Mistress Prudence, Mrs. Clifford.

The house was crowded to excess before the curtain rose. At the end of the first act, according to the *Era*, the public were disappointed, and wondered a stronger impression had not been made upon them by a play of Bulwer's. "Had the author been altogether unknown," says this paper, "we have some suspicion that their surprise would have been expressed in a very unequivocal manner. They remembered, however, that Bulwer was a successful dramatist, and beyond all question a man of genius, and they saw before them on the stage a constellation of talent such as could be produced at no other

theatre in London. The interest opened in the
second act, and increased, though only a little, in
the third; but in the fourth this slow and stately
stream of passion acquired the impetuosity of a
torrent, and the drop scene fell amidst thunders
of applause. Such profound emotion could not
be increased by any human skill in the fifth act,
but this department of the piece, although the
*dénouement* occupied too much time, was sufficiently well managed to prevent any sensible
flagging of the interest, and the curtain closed upon
one of the most successful pieces (so far as may be
argued from a first representation) we ever saw."

At the fall of the curtain Macready was called,
and on his appearance bouquets and laurel-
wreaths were thrown on the stage. Then Mrs.
Warner and Miss Faucit were summoned to
receive enthusiastic applause, after which Bulwer's
presence was demanded. Concerning this the
*Morning Post* states: " The playwright responded
by ' putting his head out of his box and bowing
genteelly to the audience.' "

Not proving a success the piece was soon withdrawn. Subsequently it was rewritten, and under

the name of *The Rightful Heir* was produced on
the 3rd October, 1868, at the Lyceum Theatre,
with a cast which included Messrs. Hermann
Vezin, Henry Neville, Lawlor, George Peel, Band-
mann, Lin Rayne, T. Anderson, Dan Evans, Basil
Potter, Everard, Mrs. H. Vezin, and Miss M.
Palmer. It was played for a limited number of
nights.

The author's next dramatic venture was the
comedy of *Money*, first produced on the 8th of
December, 1840. Before that date Macready
had ended a short engagement at Drury Lane
Theatre, and returned to the Haymarket on
the 16th of March of that year. The while
Sir Edward Lytton Bulwer was busy writing
*Money*, and in October placed it in Macready's
hands. In accordance with his usual custom the
latter was unsparing in his efforts towards ensuring
the comedy's success, rehearsing it repeatedly ; at
one time devoting two hours' labour to a single
page, and learning to play piquet that his manner
might appear natural in the gambling scene.
And as he strove sorrow abided with him, for his
blessed and beloved Joan, his light of life, his

little daughter aged three, sickened and died.
Within a week from the day she was laid at
rest, *Money* was announced for performance, and
Macready took his way to the playhouse heavy-
hearted.

The following cast appeared in the original
performance :

| | |
|---|---|
| Lord Glossmore . . . . . | MR. VINING. |
| Sir John Vesey . . . . . | MR. STRICKLAND. |
| Sir Frederick Blount . . . | MR. LACY. |
| Stout . . . . . . | MR. D. REES. |
| Graves . . . . . . | MR. WEBSTER. |
| Evelyn . . . . . . | MR. MACREADY. |
| Captain Dudley Smooth . . . | MR. WRENCH. |
| Sharp . . . . . . | MR. WALDRON. |
| Toke. . . . . . . | MR. OXBERRY. |
| Frantz (Tailor) . . . . . | MR. O. SMITH. |
| Tabouret (Upholsterer) . . . | MR. HOWE. |
| MacFinch (Jeweller) . . . | MR. GOUGH. |
| MacStucco (Architect) . . . | MR. MATHEWS. |
| Kite (Horse-dealer) . . . . | MR. SAUTER. |
| Crimson (Portrait-painter) . . | MR. GALLOT. |
| Grub (Publisher) . . . . | MR. CAULFIELD. |
| Patent (Coach-builder) . . . | MR. CLARKE. |
| Lady Franklin . . . . . | MRS. GLOVER. |
| Georgina (Daughter to Sir John) . | MISS HORTON. |
| Clara (Companion to Lady Franklin) | MISS FAUCIT. |

No sooner were the doors of the Haymarket
Theatre opened on the evening of the 8th of

December, 1840, than the house was crowded in
every part. The strongest indications of impatience for the rise of the curtain were manifested
in all directions. At last the overture ended and
the play began. The first acts were well received,
but the *Times* states during the fourth act many
of the audience began to hiss strongly. However,
this sign of disapproval was soon subdued, and at
the conclusion the house was uproariously enthusiastic. Macready and Miss Faucit were called
before the curtain, after which Sir Lytton Bulwer
was summoned in the same manner. In answer
to this Webster came forward and said Sir Edward
had left the house. Dissatisfied with his reply the
audience shouted, " Bring him back, where did he
go ? " to which Webster made no reply, when
general confusion ensued and the peacefully disposed quickly retired. Bearing recent experiences
in our minds it is interesting to hear the *Times*
comment, forty-six years ago, on the conduct of
audiences flocking to witness premier representations. " These violent first-night demonstrations,"
says that journal, "are now too well known to be
taken as of any value." Speaking of the play the

same authority was of opinion, the leading idea
of the piece that friends come and go with wealth
and poverty was trite, and that the expedient of
trying real and false friends was one of the most
common.   The satire was not remarkably pungent;
the sentimental language seldom rose above the
commonplaces usually spoken by the interesting
heroes of dramas and novels.   The dialogue
amused by an occasional oddity, a quaint saying;
a happy expression of some home truth ; but there
was no brilliancy, though occasionally such was
attempted.   The merit of the piece really lay in
the construction of certain scenes, where a great
number of persons could be combined with effect.
The reading of the will, the bustle of the club-
room, with the dovetailing of speeches of
various personages, evinced talent, and that in
a difficult part of dramatic construction.   To this
was the favourable reception of the drama greatly
to be attributed, as likewise to the termination of
the story ; since although that was not particularly
ingenious, the preference of an affectionate young
lady to one who merely seeks for a fortune must
be pleasing ; and the sentiment that a man is

really worth more than his money, must, however conveyed, command a certain portion of applause.

The play drew crowded houses night after night, and ran at the Haymarket Theatre until the end of Macready's engagement, the 15th March, 1841.

Sir Edward Lytton Bulwer having succeeded as a dramatist, and contradicted the prognostications of his critics, rested from further efforts in this branch of art for upwards of eleven years. At the end of that period he wrote a comedy in five acts entitled *Not so Bad as We Seem*; or, *Many Sides to a Character*, for a company of amateur actors bearing well-known names; who, by the performance of this play, raised funds for the establishment of The Guild of Literature and Art. The purpose of the association was to encourage life assurance and other provident habits among authors and artists; to render such assistance to both as shall never compromise their independence; and to found a new institution where honourable rest from arduous labour shall still be associated with the discharge of congenial duties. The characters of the comedy played for the establishment of this worthy guild were sustained by the following notable cast:

| | |
|---|---|
| The Duke of Middlesex . . | MR. FRANK STONE. |
| The Earl of Loftus . . . | MR. DUDLEY COSTELLO. |
| Lord Wilmot (his Son) . . | MR. CHARLES DICKENS. |
| Mr. Shadowly Softhead . . | MR. DOUGLAS JERROLD. |
| Mr. Hardman . . . . | MR. JOHN FORSTER. |
| Sir Geoffrey Thornside . . | MR. MARK LEMON. |
| Mr. Goodenough Easy . . | MR. F. TOPHAM. |
| Lord Le Trimmer . . . | MR. PETER CUNNINGHAM. |
| Sir Thomas Timid . . . | MR. WESTLAND MARSTON. |
| Colonel Flint . . . . | MR. R. H. HORNE. |
| Mr. Jacob Tonson . . . | MR. CHARLES KNIGHT. |
| Smart (Valet to Lord Wilmot) | MR. WILKIE COLLINS. |
| Hodge (Servant to Sir Geoffrey) | MR. JOHN TENNIEL. |
| Paddy O'Sullivan . . . | MR. ROBERT BELL. |
| Mr. David Fallen . . . | MR. AUGUSTUS EGG, A.R.A. |
| Lucy (Daughter to Sir Geoffrey) | MRS. COMPTON. |
| Barbara (Daughter to Mr. Easy) | MISS ELLEN CHAPLIN. |

Scenes for the comedy were painted, and presented as free-will offerings by Stanfield, David Roberts, Thomas Grieve, Telbin, Absolon, and Louis Haghe. A portable theatre was built for the occasion, and set up in the library of Devonshire House, kindly lent by the Duke of Devonshire, a man of kindliest nature, who felt deep interest in all connected with literature and art. Great expectations were entertained regarding the comedy, and the highest curiosity obtained to witness the performance of such distinguished amateurs. Tickets of admission were five guineas each ; the Queen sent a hundred guineas for a box. Accordingly on the 14th of May, 1851, the date on which *Not so Bad as We Seem* was first performed, the picture gallery of Devonshire House, which, adjoining the library, served as an auditorium, was crowded with a singularly brilliant audience.

Her Majesty, the Prince Consort, the Prince and Princess of Prussia, the Duke of Wellington, the Russian, Prussian, Sardinian, and American Ministers, together with some of the most distinguished peers and peeresses in the realm were present; whilst the aristocracy of talent was represented by Lady Morgan, the Hon. Mrs. Norton, Sir Edward Bulwer Lytton, Monckton Milnes, Thomas Babington Macaulay, Mr. Justice Talfourd, and Harrison Ainsworth. At nine o'clock the Duke of Devonshire's excellent band played an overture expressly composed for the occasion by His Grace's private pianist, Mr. Charles Coote. On its conclusion the curtain

Y

ascended and the play began. Every scene was received with applause. The actors enjoyed their work no less than the audience approved their efforts. Both were so close together, as Mr. Charles Knight writes, "that as Mr. Jacob Tonson sat in Wills' Coffee House, he could have touched, with his clouded cane, the Duke of Wellington who was of Her Majesty's suite." The performance being a splendid success, the play was transferred to the Hanover Square Rooms, where it was repeated to crowded houses throughout the hot nights of June and July. Later on the comedy, represented by almost the same cast, was taken into the provinces, when thousands crowded to see the play and players. Many were the adventures and strange the occurrences which befel the latter. One evening when they were about to appear at Bath, their perruquier suddenly rushed to where the amateurs had assembled, and with a look of horror announced their wigs had not arrived. The hairdressers' shops were searched in vain. "The time," writes Charles Knight, "was long past when Bath could produce a stock of perukes such as were the glory of the

days of Nash. It was a question whether our
Duke of Middlesex, our Earl Loftus, and our
Lord Wilmot could be content with the scratch
wigs of our own degenerate days, or appear in
their gorgeous array of velvet and lace with their
own cropped hair. We really dreaded for our
poor perruquier some such catastrophe as happened to the cook of Louis XIV. when the fish
came too late for dinner. But the fates were
propitious. The wigs arrived at the last moment."

Everywhere the distinguished amateurs met
with success ; the play ran like wild-fire. "We
have had prodigious houses," writes Dickens to
Forster from Sunderland. "Into the room at
Newcastle (where Lord Carlisle was, by-the-bye)
they squeezed six hundred people, at twelve and
sixpence, into a space reasonably capable of holding three hundred. Last night, in a hall built
like a theatre, with pit, boxes, and gallery, we
had about twelve hundred, I dare say more. They
began with a round of applause when Coote's
white waistcoat appeared on the orchestra, and
wound up the farce with three deafening cheers.
I never saw such good fellows."

Sufficient money for establishing the Guild of Literature and Art was obtained ; but the institution, after a brief existence, failed for lack of subsequent support.

The last dramatic work from Lord Lytton's pen which the public has seen is *Junius; or, The Household Gods*. This piece was produced at the Princess's Theatre, under management of Mr. Wilson Barrett. A brilliant audience, including the Prince and Princess of Wales, and many men and women of note in literature and art, assembled on the evening of February 26th, 1885, to witness its first representation. All was accomplished that the ability of its performers, the skill of scenic artists, and the labour of mechanicians could achieve towards rendering *Junius* successful.

Picturesque and impressive, by reason of its interpretation and setting rather than from its strength and resources, it pleased the sight rather than satisfied the judgment of its spectators. From the hearty applause greeting every scene, and the stormy enthusiasm awarding its conclusion, it might be considered a desired result had been attained. But on calmer consideration and repeated performance the play was seen to be unworthy the efforts and money devoted to its production. In a brace of concise sentences the *Athenæum* gave voice to a general verdict regarding its merits. "Lord Lytton's new drama," says that journal, "is exactly what might have been and was anticipated. It is a clever and artificial work, in which the action is all but dramatic, and the dialogue rhetorical."

It was withdrawn from the stage of the Princess's Theatre on the 28th of March, a month and two days from the date of its first production.

THE END.

CHARLES DICKENS AND EVANS, CRYSTAL PALACE PRESS.